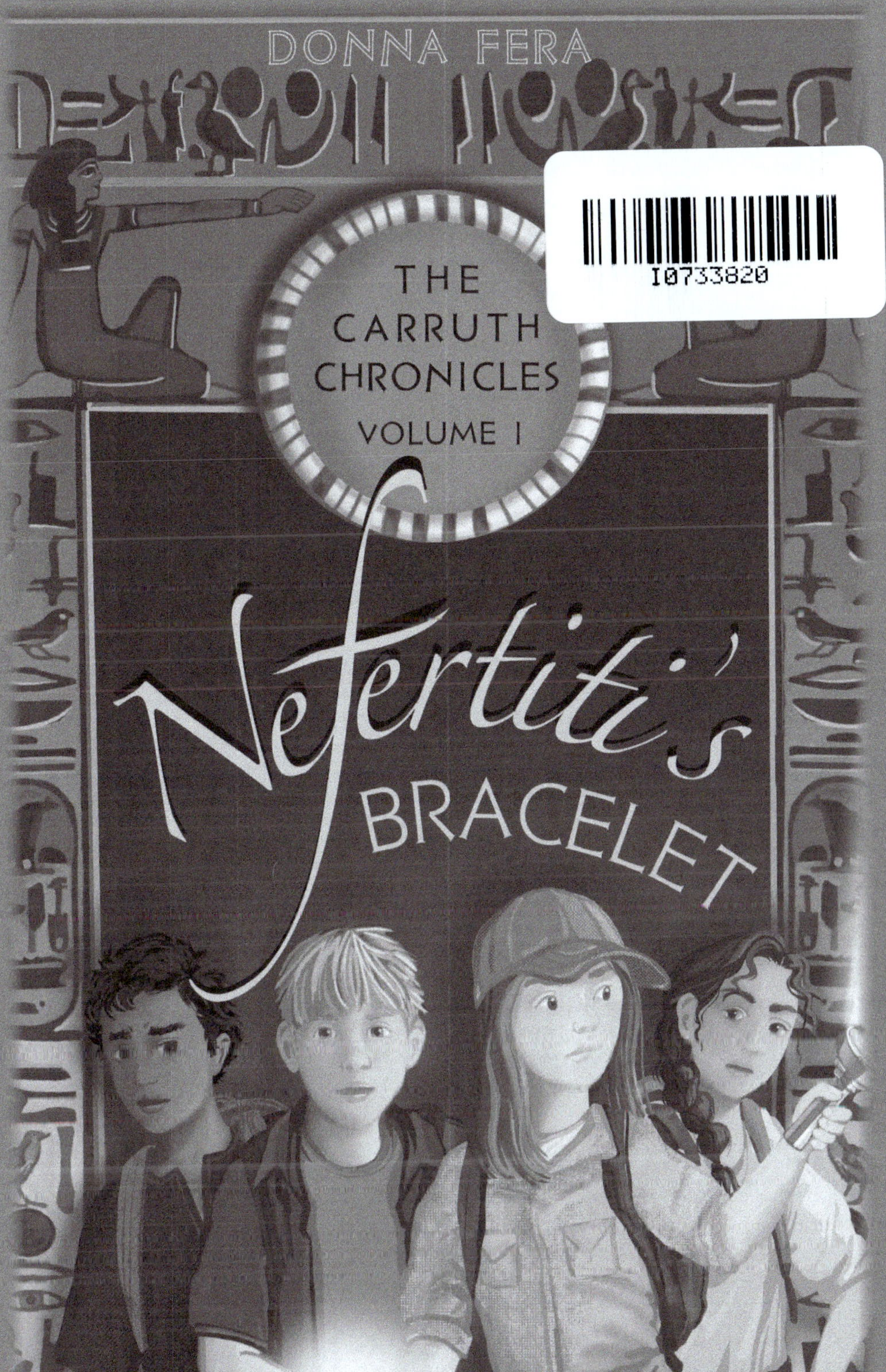
DONNA FERA
THE
CARRUTH
CHRONICLES
VOLUME I
Nefertiti's
BRACELET

To Suzi and Tyler
for your constant
support and encouragement.
I Love You!
Mom

1

London, England
One year ago

"Sir . . . Sir! . . . you dropped this . . ." The young boy chased down the older gentleman as he made his way quickly through the crowded market-filled streets of the Portobello district in London. The older man seemed distracted and obviously in a terrible hurry.

"Oh yes, yes. It seems I did." The man took the small bag he'd dropped, nodded a courteous thank you, then placed a single quid in the boy's hand, swiftly continuing on his way.

The market bustled with anxious workers heading off to tend to the day's business. Much of the market consisted of old antique shops, bookstores, collectors' shops, and trendy markets.

Nicholas McIntyre stopped briefly to look toward the old antique shop just up the way. "Good morning, Mister McIntyre, sir," the nearby fruit vendor said.

Nicholas turned toward the vendor. "Good morning, Thomas. A fine assortment of fruit you have today."

"Thank you. Thank you, sir. What brings you to the dodgy end of the market this fine morning?"

Nicholas chuckled and responded with a wink as he picked up a fine red apple. "I have a little trinket I would like Miles to have a look at. Do you know if his shop is open today?" he said as he rooted around in his trouser pocket for a few coins to pay Thomas. Miles Moore's Magnificent Marvels was a collector's haven of rare artifacts and collectibles. Miles was especially versed in ancient Egyptian artifacts and culture and had once worked for the Cairo Museum of Antiquities.

"I think so. I just saw him only a moment ago heading down the street," Thomas replied.

"Excellent, excellent. I will head there straight away then." Nicholas placed the coins in Thomas's hand. "Thank you, Thomas. You have yourself a wonderful day, and give Molly my regards."

"Will do, sir. You do the same."

Nicholas McIntyre waved goodbye to his old friend and headed down the street.

Moments later, another man approached Thomas' stand. "That man, what did he want?" The man demanded in a harsh French accent.

"I beg your pardon, sir . . . What man?" Thomas replied.

"You heard me, you imbecile! What did he want?"

Thomas was taken aback by the man's insistence and refused to answer. "I have no idea who or what you are talking about, sir," he said defiantly.

Angry and frustrated, the stranger knocked Thomas' fruit stand over and ran away.

Ten minutes passed, and as Thomas was busy cleaning up the mess the stranger had so kindly left him, a woman's scream pierced the otherwise peaceful morning. Within minutes, people began to crowd around Miles' shop. Thomas ran quickly to see what all the commotion was about. But when Thomas and several other street vendors approached, they saw Nicholas McIntyre leaning against the door of Miles' shop. He had a dagger protruding from his back, and his jacket had been ransacked.

Horrified, Thomas dropped to his knees to help his old friend. "No! Mr. McIntyre, sir! Stay with me! Hold on!" But it was too late. Nicholas McIntyre was dead.

It wasn't long before sirens rang out, and detectives from Scotland Yard arrived on the scene. Moments later, Miles approached the old antique shop he called his home away from home. He could barely even see his shop for the crowds of people hovering around his door.

"What on earth?" Miles exclaimed as he pushed through the crowd. Suddenly, he saw his old friend lying motionless next to his door. Devastated, Miles asked, "Nicholas! Oh, good Lord! What happened'?"

He'd only stepped away momentarily to retrieve the morning newspaper and a cup of tea. "How could this be?" Miles looked up at his friend, Thomas. "Nick called me just last week. He had something he wanted me to look over for him." The detective who'd been standing nearby helped Miles as he sat slowly down on a bench next to the front door of his shop. Devastated, he continued, "He wanted my opinion on its authenticity." Thomas sat and comforted his old friend as the detective questioned Miles about his knowledge of Mr. McIntyre's visit to his shop.

"Do you know if that is why he came here this morning, Mr. Moore?" asked the plump detective as he scribbled notes on his tiny notepad.

"I would guess so . . . we are good friends, but he rarely comes into the shop unless he has something he needs me to authenticate," Miles responded breathlessly, still in shock over the event that had just taken place.

Thomas chimed in. "Officer, yes, as a matter of fact, he did come here to show something to Miles." Thomas went on to explain the earlier discussion he and Nicholas had regarding the "trinket" Nicholas wanted Miles to examine. He also explained about the strange Frenchman who approached him shortly after asking questions and demolished his fruit stand.

"Thank you . . . Thomas, is it? You've been quite helpful. We will let you gentlemen know once we've located this man's killer."

"Thank you, Inspector, and I'd like to press charges for damages to my fruit stand, too!" Thomas exclaimed as the inspector walked away.

The investigation of the murder went on well into the afternoon. Seated in the shadows of a small sidewalk café across the street, a woman quietly watched over the investigation. A black and gray Hermès scarf hid most of her face, except for her piercing blue eyes, which peered over the edge.

2

Charlotte, North Carolina

Spring had begun to blossom everywhere in North Carolina. The Carolina blue sky was bright, and flowering azaleas were scattered across the suburbs like a beautiful French painting. For most kids, spring signified the end of the school year was quickly approaching. Excited students began to plan for vacations, summer camps, and trips to the closest lake or beach. For the Carruth children, however, late spring brought adventure and excitement that most kids only dreamed of or read about in books. This summer, the Carruths planned to spend most of their summer break in a tomb just outside Cairo, Egypt. Their mother, Dr. Eleanor "Ellie" Carruth, PhD, was an archaeology professor at the university. She spent her summers digging and searching for historical artifacts at some of the world's most remote and exotic locations. The university sponsored most of her projects, and she worked directly with museums and governments all over the world to recover these unusual and fascinating artifacts. This particular summer, the excavation of history's treasures was partnered with the Cairo Museum of Antiquities. Ellie and her late husband, Dr. Jason Carruth, PhD, had worked with the Cairo Museum many times in the past, and this was Ellie's first time back since the untimely death of her husband. As such, she looked forward to this new assignment. Ellie felt it was time to get herself and her two children back to what was *their* normal.

Ellie Carruth was not the only one excited about this new assignment. Ellie's oldest, Suzi, and her younger brother, Tyler, accompanied their mother every June. Suzi loved going on these digs and absolutely looked forward to it every year. Tyler enjoyed it as well; however, his taste for American food and the fact that he didn't get to play in the summer hockey league made him less excited about it than his sister. At age fourteen, this made Suzi's sixth trip; she was now quite a veteran. Tyler was thirteen, and this would be his fifth trip. Although still young, the Carruth siblings were very seasoned travelers and well-accustomed to the rigors of a trek through the desert. After all, they had as much experience as many of the adults on these projects. The truth was, they knew just enough to get themselves into mischief. And lots of it!

"Woo hoo! Two more weeks till we leave for Cairo!" Suzi exclaimed as she burst into the kitchen where her mother was putting away the groceries.

"Yes, two weeks. Did you empty the dishwasher like I asked?" her mother asked.

"Yep!" Suzi continued, as she scurried happily around, helping her mother with the groceries. "I can't wait to see Naeem! His dad said he could go with us again. I can't believe it, the Valley of the Queens! Naeem said he knows about a great cave near the dig site that we can explore!" Suzi rattled on. She was so excited and could hardly contain herself.

"Whoa, just hold on!" Ellie stopped in the middle of the kitchen and looked squarely at her daughter. "The Cairo Museum wants me to investigate a possible tomb. This is a really important dig, and we could use your help. Besides, I don't want you all wandering off," Ellie continued and returned to her mission of finding a spot for the cereal in the pantry. "You know how dangerous it can get out there."

"But Mom!"

"No buts, Suz. You guys need to stay close to camp. Period!"

"Hppfft . . . close-ish," Suzi grumbled to herself with a frustrated roll of her eyes.

"I'm serious, Suzanna. We're not even completely sure where this tomb is, and there's evidence that it may have been raided. I do not want you kids running around outside of the perimeter. It could be dangerous if these raiders are still hanging around."

The house phone rang, saving Ellie from further discussion with her daughter about the matter.

"I'll get the phone, Suz. You go finish your homework," her mother demanded as she lifted the phone receiver. "Hello?"

"Algebra . . . Woohoo!" Suzi mumbled to herself as she left the kitchen.

"Dr. Eleanor Carruth, please," requested the voice from the phone.

"Yes. This is Eleanor Carruth. How may I help you?"

"I am Dr. Asim Nasar. From the Cairo Museum of Antiquities. I have been asked to contact you regarding your next assignment," explained the voice on the phone.

"Oh . . . Okay. I'm afraid I'm not familiar with you, Dr. Nasar. Are you new to the Museum?" Ellie replied.

"Yes, as a matter of fact, I am. I joined the museum's excavation team only three months ago," Nasar replied.

"That's excellent! And please, call me Ellie. What do you need from me?" Dr. Carruth replied.

"We have your flight booked out of Charlotte, North Carolina, on Tuesday, the 15th. You will be leaving on American Airlines flight 1260 to London. Your flight will arrive at

Heathrow Airport. Is that okay with you?" asked Dr. Nasar.

"That sounds good," Ellie replied.

"Great! From there, you will board British Airways Flight 5789 from London to Cairo. We will have Ahmal Patier meet you there by car."

"Good 'ol Ahmal," Ellie added.

"Ahmal is a good man." Nasar continued, "Now, Dr. Carruth . . . are you aware of the nature of this project?"

"I believe so. I was told there are certain complications surrounding the digging site," Ellie responded quietly. She looked down the hallway to make sure Suzi was not listening in on her conversation. "I know the site has been compromised and that items may have been removed. I was also told by your predecessor that we may need to be more cautious than normal this time."

"This is correct. I encourage you to use extreme caution this time, Dr. Carruth. I have arranged for a few extra men to be on hand for added security."

"We definitely will. Are you joining us on this trip, Dr. Nasar?"

"Yes, I am actually looking forward to it. I was not given these 'on location' opportunities with my last assignment in Alexandria. When my wife passed, I made the decision to stay home with my daughter. Now that she is older, it is exciting to return to doing what I love so much." Nasar continued, "Since I have not been on a dig in many years, I am looking forward to being a part of this project."

"Excellent! I look forward to working with you. Okay, so . . . let's get started. What additional project information do you have for me?" Ellie sat down at the kitchen desk, pulled out a notepad, and began taking notes. The phone call lasted about twenty minutes. She couldn't quite put her finger on it, but there was something with this assignment that unnerved her slightly. Perhaps it was nothing, but just in case, she planned to say very little to the kids about it, especially Suzi.

Back in the family library, Suzi found herself a bit distracted after finishing the last few problems of her Algebra homework.

"Suzi? Where are you?" her mother called out.

"In here," Suzi replied.

"There you are," Ellie said as she tripped over mounds of backpacks, utensils, and various excavation tools. "Ugh! This mess! Did you finish your Algebra?" Ellie shifted a small stack of books out of her way. "Have you started packing?"

"Seriously, Mom? I packed it a week ago. And yes. I finished my homework," Suzi casually remarked, barely looking up from her computer.

Ellie moved another larger stack of books over to the corner. "What are you doing in here anyway? It's a mess!"

"Reading about the Valley of the Queens," Suzi answered again without looking up from her computer.

"Uh-huh, and I suppose studying Algebra would be out of the question," her mother said, knowing full well that Egypt trumped Algebra any day.

"Mom, I did my homework and studied for my final exam."

"Yeah, well, that C on your midterm tells me you may need more than just a few minutes of review." Suzanna's grades were always excellent, except in Algebra. Where math was concerned, Ellie had to just accept the grades her daughter brought home and let it go. The A's she received in every other subject were solid enough.

The Carruth family library was large and looked like a time capsule that made a stop in every historical time period from 2,500 B.C. to today. There were artifacts from every archaeological dig Ellie and her late husband, Jason, had been part of for the last twenty years. In one corner, there were six stacks of books. Each stack stood close to four feet tall. One entire stack alone was strictly about Egypt. The library was complete with an antique desk and oversized scenic windows that boasted a relaxing view of beautiful rolling pastures where the Carruth's horses spent their days. Floor-to-ceiling shelves surrounded much of the room and housed hundreds of books, files, boxes, and artifacts from civilizations all over the globe. Truthfully, the room was a disaster and in dire need of organization. Dr. Carruth once asked their housekeeper, Stella, to help go through the room to get it organized, but Stella left screaming in Spanish. She spoke perfect English, and since she was yelling in Spanish, Ellie felt it best to let it go and never ask again. This was one of her best decisions, by the way, and the room stayed a mess.

All the files for the dig and the Carruth travel documents arrived by FedEx a week later. While her mother was busy tending to last-minute arrangements with the University and finding someone to care for the farm and their horses, Suzi could only think of what awaited them at the Valley of the Queens. It was the adventure Suzi had looked forward to for six months. Egypt was Suzi's favorite. She had been all over the world, but the Great Wall of China was nothing compared to the ancient ruins of Egypt. There was something about Egypt Suzi couldn't quite explain. Perhaps it was the mystery behind every wall or the feeling that 3,000 years of pharaohs and their queens seemed to call out to her. Or, it might be that Egypt was the last place she worked with *both* her parents. Before her father died a year ago, he often encouraged her inquisitive ways and even defended her when her mother wanted to rein her in at times. Whatever it was, Suzi was up for the challenge. She loved Egypt, and Egypt loved her.

The morning they were to leave, the Carruth household was in chaos, as always. "Suz! Ty! The taxi is here, let's go! Hurry, or we'll miss the flight," Ellie called out to her children as she scrambled around, trying to gather their bags.

"Mom! I can't find my phone!" Tyler fussed.

Suzi handed him his phone as she whizzed past them, heading straight for the taxi. "I have it; it was in the bathroom. Why was it in there, by the way? Nope . . . wait . . . never mind, I don't want to know."

Tyler followed his sister out the door. "What? I was brushing my teeth!"

"Okay . . . Does everybody have everything? Get it now because we are not turning this taxi around if you forgot something!" Ellie declared as she stood in the doorway, recalling her previous experience.

"Mom, we have everything! Let's go!" Suzi yelled back from the door of the taxi. She could hardly contain herself. She'd barely slept the night before and finally dozed off somewhere around 2 a.m. out of sheer exhaustion.

Ellie closed the front door and approached the rear of the taxi. The driver loaded the few pieces of luggage and then looked around for more bags. But Ellie simply winked at the driver and smiled, "We have to travel light this time." The driver gave a relieved nod and shut the trunk.

As they drove off and their beautiful farm became smaller in the rearview mirror, Ellie had that weird feeling again. She'd recently called an old friend she had worked with many times to join her on the upcoming project. Her friend agreed but seemed strangely preoccupied. In the past, they would meet in the London airport and fly to Cairo together. The flight was a great opportunity to discuss the project and its timeline. But this time, her friend and colleague, Mandi, was distracted and said she would just meet them in Cairo. They could review the information then. *Odd*, Dr. Carruth thought to herself. *Really odd.*

3

Casablanca, Morocco

On a stormy evening in the large library of a Moroccan castle, an older, distinguished gentleman waited anxiously. He sat, shifting nervously, in a large brown leather chair. A gold chain with a small gold and lapis cartouche left a mark in the palm of his hand as he held it firmly. The cartouche belonged to an ancient Egyptian royal family and bore the name of a mysterious pharaoh. The lights flickered, and he stood and walked toward the window to look out into the storm. A bold flash of lightning lit up the library from outside. A knock on the study door caught his attention as he peered out the giant window into the rainy evening.

"Come in," he turned and said anxiously.

A tall, athletic woman with sleek, long black hair entered the room. Her olive skin contrasted with the cobalt blue eyes that peered from underneath the black bangs that fell neatly on her forehead.

"Ah, Mandisa. Come in, my dear. Have a seat," the old man offered.

She walked across the room. "I have the bracelet." The woman handed a small linen pouch to the man as she sat in the chair next to him.

The pouch itself was stunning. It was made of deep purple linen and encrusted with gold thread and emerald beads. Small rubies outlined the edges of the bag. Hieroglyphics painted in fourteen-carat gold on the outside gave clues to the bag's origin and what it might contain.

Using a handkerchief, and careful not to touch the actual object inside, the old man pulled the delicate gold and lapis bracelet from the pouch. He then held it up to the light to look at its magnificence. "Excellent. How did you manage to retrieve it?" he asked as he compared the hieroglyphics to the cartouche he had been holding.

"It was a bit tricky. Unfortunately, Mr. McIntyre met an untimely death at the hands of a French antiquities dealer before I could talk to him. Later that evening, as the Frenchman slept, I slipped into his hotel room and relieved him of his prize," she said proudly.

"I knew Nicholas McIntyre; he was a good man. I hate that the Frenchman got to him before we did. I feel sure Nicholas would have seen our point of view. I know he wanted to prove he'd found the queen, but I am sure he would have listened to us in the end." The man continued, "Do you think the Frenchman was with the 'Network?'"

"It's possible," the woman replied.

"Well then, we must go to Egypt and place this in its rightful home. Have Timmons arrange for my jet," he said decisively.

"When do you wish to leave?" she asked.

"First thing in the morning. Besides, I am sure Ellie will be looking for your assistance on this excavation the museum has set up," the old man said.

The woman smiled and nodded. "Yes, she called a few weeks ago to make sure I would be working with the team again. Father, she is good. She will find her."

"Yes, my dear; I know. We will have to deal with that when, or if, the time comes."

The woman left quietly as the old man turned back toward

the window to contemplate his morning journey and the important task at hand.

4

Charlotte-Douglas International Airport
Charlotte, NC

"American Airlines Flight 1260 . . . service from Charlotte to London's Heathrow Airport." A voice announced over the loudspeaker in the terminal. *"Now boarding at Gate D3."*

Tyler woke from a short snooze. "Uggh!" He stretched. "I'm not looking forward to this long flight!"

"I know, hon, but you'll be fine," Ellie replied.

Suzi chimed in with her typical adventurous enthusiasm, "It'll be fun! The gate agent said they have several good in-flight movies available."

"Easy for you to say. You weren't sitting next to some big, gross dude with serious stomach issues last time," Tyler whined. "Every time I moved, he'd shift and fart. It was so nasty!"

Suzi snickered.

Ellie reassured her son that this had happened only once, and he would be sitting next to her, as usual, on this flight. They would not be separated again. The three of them boarded the Boeing 777, and as promised, they were all three sitting together with her between the two of them.

Heathrow International Airport
London, England

By the time they reached London, their flight to Cairo was delayed, and they would be stuck in the London airport for the next two hours. Tyler and his mom took advantage of the break and fell fast asleep on a couch in the boarding area. Suzi, on the other hand, helped herself to her mother's briefcase and took out the notes on the upcoming project and a bag of Hershey's Kisses. Suzi read intently while enjoying a good amount of chocolate. Soon, she noticed an Egyptian girl about her own age seated across the boarding area. Suzi continued to read her mother's notes, with only an occasional glance across the room. Eventually, she noticed the girl looking back at her, and it wasn't long before Suzi boldly decided to introduce herself. After all, the girl was all alone, and it was obvious they were both going to the same place, Cairo.

"Hi," Suzi said as she approached the young girl. "Umm . . . want some chocolate?" Suzi presented the open and well-eaten bag of Hershey's Kisses.

The girl simply stared back at her, cautiously taking a sip from her water bottle. Suzi wondered if she spoke English or Arabic. Unsure what to do, Suzi made a clumsy attempt to speak to her in Arabic but ended up asking her if she rode a camel to the toilet. The girl laughed so hard that she spit out the water she'd just sipped.

"Maaaann, I have *got* to start listening to Naeem when he's trying to teach me this stuff!" Exasperated, Suzi plopped down in the seat next to her.

Still giggling, the girl stuck out her hand and said, "Hi, I am Emma."

"Suzi," she said and shook Emma's hand in return.

"I am sorry for not speaking at first." Emma reached into the bag of Hershey's Kisses and grabbed a few pieces of chocolate. "My aunt warned me not to talk to strangers in the airports, but anyone who tried that hard to speak to me in Arabic cannot be too bad."

Slightly embarrassed, Suzi shifted in her seat. "My friend Naeem always tries to teach me, but I never listen."

"Perhaps you should," Emma replied, still giggling. "Do you have any idea what you said?"

"No, not really. Do I wanna know?"

"No, not really," said Emma.

"Okay, maybe not." Suzi sighed, then asked, "Are you going to Cairo?"

"Yes, I am going home. I have been visiting family in America."

"Oh really? Where?" Suzi asked excitedly.

Emma's eyes opened wide, and she took a deep breath as she told Suzi, "Some place called Las Vegas, Nevada."

"Ha! Vegas? Really?" Now, it was Suzi's turn to giggle. "How was that?" Suzi knew what Egyptian customs were like and was completely shocked by the fact that Emma had family who lived in Las Vegas, of all places. "Are these American relatives?"

"No, my aunt and uncle moved there from Alexandria when my uncle's job transferred him to America." Emma just looked at Suzi with a blank stare as she continued to tell her about what she saw on the Vegas Strip.

"There were women with almost no clothes on, lots of them. They wore feathers, lots and lots of feathers. Feathers every where. Lights everywhere." Still looking horrified, she continued to rattle on about a man in a show that was attacked by a tiger. "What was he thinking, playing with a tiger?"

"Actually, I heard about that on the news," Suzi chimed in. "Did you see the Luxor Hotel?"

"I did, yes," Emma quietly replied but said nothing else.

Suzi actually felt bad for Emma. Knowing how the Egyptians feel about their past and traditions, Suzi asked, "How do your aunt and uncle feel about living there?"

"Seriously? They told me to *relax*! America is a great place to live. So many opportunities, so many possibilities."

"I'm really sorry. The rest of the States aren't like that though . . . " Suzi was interrupted by the boarding announcement.

"British Airways Flight 5789 to Cairo will be ready for boarding in approximately five minutes."

"Well, Emma, I should probably return to my mom and brother. It was really nice to meet you."

"You too. And thanks for the chocolate!" Emma waved.

Suzi rushed over to stash her mother's notes back into her briefcase before she woke up. She was just in time! The Carruths quickly gathered their bags and walked to the gate. Just before boarding the aircraft herself, Emma waved back at her new friend and then disappeared onto the jetway.

Once on board, the Carruths situated themselves in their usual order: Tyler preferred the window, Suzi was on the aisle, and Ellie nestled between them.

"Welcome aboard British Airways Flight 5789, with non-stop service to Cairo, Egypt. We are approaching 35,000 feet, and it should be a smooth flight this morning. The flight attendants will be around shortly with the in-flight service."

"Suzi, who's that girl you waved to in the terminal?" Ellie asked.

"Her name is Emma! She's from Egypt and was visiting her aunt and uncle back in the States. They live in Las Vegas, of all places!" Suzi giggled.

"I'm sorry, did you say Vegas?" Ellie turned to Suzi.

"Yeah, she hated it!" Suzi continued to snicker as she reached for a book from her bag.

"Oh, I'm sure she did!" Ellie agreed with a slight giggle herself.

Suzi looked back at Emma, who was sitting only a few rows behind them. "Mom, is it okay if Emma comes up and takes this extra seat across the aisle?"

"Sure, if it is okay with the flight attendant," Ellie replied.

Suzi asked the attendant, who agreed, so off Suzi went to retrieve her new friend.

"Emma, this is my mom. Mom, this is Emma."

"Hi, Emma. It's nice to meet you." Ellie reached to shake Emma's hand. "I'm Ellie Carruth, and this is . . . uh . . . well, Suzi's brother, Ty." Tyler sat snoring and slumped over halfway in the seat with his legs stretched out under the seat in front of him.

Emma sat down across from Suzi, and they talked the entire five-hour flight. They talked about the U.S. and what it was really like. They talked about Egypt and how they could maybe hang out a little while they were in Cairo, when she was done with the project they came to work on, of course.

Ellie looked out the window and saw the Pyramids of Giza in the distance. "Suzi, honey, it looks like we're coming into Cairo. Put your things away and get settled in," she instructed.

Suzi leaned over and whispered to Emma. "I think my mom secretly wanted to be a flight attendant," she joked.

The two giggled and then did as they were told.

Just then, a voice said, *"Attention, Ladies and Gentlemen: we are descending through 10,000 feet and will land in Cairo shortly. Please fasten your seat belts. Flight attendants. Pre-*

pare the cabin for landing. It looks like it will be a pleasant afternoon in Cairo today."

5

Cairo International Airport
Cairo, Egypt

The Cairo Airport was a large and crowded connection point for many flights across the globe and the midway point to many destinations between Europe, Africa, and Asia.

"Dr. Carruth! Hello!" A voice from the crowd called out.

"Ahmal! So good to see you!" Ellie embraced one of her oldest and dearest friends. "How've you been?"

"Ah, yes; I have been fine. You know, it is never the same around here when you leave. And always wonderfully familiar when you return. Hello there, Emma; your father asked me to pick you up with the Carruths. I see you all have met."

Suzi and Emma looked at each other. Confused, Suzi asked Emma, "How do you know Ahmal?"

"He works for my father," Emma replied. "He is the Director of Excavation at the museum here in Cairo."

"Your dad is Asim Nasar?" Ellie and Suzi responded in harmony.

Ellie cut her eyes at her daughter because Suzi's response meant only one thing: she'd been snooping in her project notes again.

"Yes, do you know him?" Emma asked with a proud smile that spread across her face.

"No, well—not really," Suzi mumbled under her breath. She then grabbed her new friend by the arm and guided her away from her mother's disapproving glare. "He called our house in North Carolina a while back to brief my mom on the archaeological dig we've come to Cairo for."

As everyone made their way through the crowded baggage claim area, Suzi wondered, "So, Emma, you never told me why your dad sent you to America."

"I went to stay with my aunt and uncle while my father settled himself in his new post." Emma continued, "He felt like I would be less bored in America than here."

Suzi laughed. "Yeah, well, Las Vegas is a lot of things, but boring isn't one of them!"

"No kidding! Oh hey, my bag is coming through now," Emma replied.

"So, where did you live before Cairo?" Suzi asked.

"Alexandria, and before that, we lived in London. I was actually born there. My mum was English. She became very ill with leukemia about six years ago. When she passed away, Dad decided it would be best for us to move to Alexandria to be close to family."

"That explains the English accent," Suzi continued. "Listen, I'm really sorry about your mom. I lost my dad and Grampa about a year ago." A reminiscent and sad tone came across Suzi as she recalled her father and what he meant to her. Emma and Suzi simply looked at one another quietly.

"Ahh ha! Here's *my* bag." Suzi pulled her bag from the conveyor. "And there's Ty's bag. I can see that ugly neon green hockey tape wrapped around his bag."

"What is hockey?" Emma asked.

"Um, well, it's a lot of ice and skates and big smelly guys trying to get a little black disc into a net. It's Ty's favorite sport." Suzi gave the bag a huge tug. "He plays all winter and would play in the summer too if we weren't traveling so much," Suzi explained as she continued to struggle to pull Ty's extremely heavy bag from the baggage belt.

"Ty! Come get your bag." Suzi got a whiff of his duffle bag. "Ugghh! What the heck, Bro? Why didn't you wash that sweaty socks smell out of that thing before you packed it? So gross! Take this thing, Tyler!" Suzi's look of disgust was something Tyler was used to. He just sighed as he grabbed the bag and replied, "Yeah, yeah. Whatever. I was busy."

Emma giggled. Since she didn't have any brothers or sisters to fight with, she found the Carruth siblings very amusing.

Suzi and Emma laughed as they grabbed their suitcases and backpacks, then walked off, realizing they might very well become lifelong friends.

Suzi soon broke the silence. "Oh hey, I can't wait to show you around! Okay, that sounds a bit strange: an American showing an Egyptian around Cairo. It'll be fun, though, I promise! I'll introduce you to Naeem. He's really cool. Ahmal is his dad," she rattled on.

Just outside the door near the arrival lane at the airport, their car, a large SUV, was waiting for them. "Hurry into the limo; we need to get going. We have to get a few things settled before we begin packing the supplies tomorrow," Ellie instructed.

As they approached the SUV, a young Egyptian boy jumped out of the back.

"Naeem!" Suzi yelled with excitement.

"Suzi! How have you been, my American friend? It is so very good to see you!" Naeem said with a great big hug. "But where is Tyler?"

"Ehh, he's pulling up the rear, as always. It's good to see you! I'm so excited. Oh my gosh, the Valley of the Queens!" Suzi exclaimed.

"And you must be Emma." Naeem reached to shake her hand. "I have heard so much about you!"

"Me? Really?" Emma was surprised.

"Yes, yes, of course. Your father speaks of you often," he replied.

"Okay, well, at least I know he missed me," Emma smiled.

Everyone piled into the large SUV that was to take them to their hotel. Tyler needed to catch up, trying to adjust his bags.

"Wait! Wait for me!" Tyler yelled as he ran after the others.

He quickly glanced behind him to ensure he hadn't left anything lying on the ground, when he noticed a sleek black Bentley that had pulled up only a few spaces behind them.

"Woah! Look at that car!" Tyler exclaimed as he jumped into the SUV. He quickly looked out the back window. "Why couldn't we have a Bentley like those guys?"

Suddenly, he noticed his ole' pal. "Yo! Naeem! What's up, dude?" The two young friends performed their secret handshake and shared a quick pat on the shoulder.

6

Cairo, Egypt

The first stop was the Ritz Carlton Hotel, just a few blocks from the Museum. The Carruths quickly checked into their hotel, dropped off their bags, and then the entire group drove to the Cairo Museum of Antiquities. Although it was definitely not the same without her father there, Suzi missed Cairo terribly and had been looking forward to returning for quite some time. Tyler also liked it, but his preference for American food over Egyptian food usually made his stay a little less exciting than Suzi's. Ellie loved this place, too. It was where she and her late husband had honeymooned . . . well, sort of. They left together on a project in Egypt right after their wedding. So, it was a working honeymoon, but neither of them minded. They loved their job, and they loved each other. The two just sort of naturally went together somehow. They were two peas in a pod and couldn't think of anywhere else they'd rather be.

So much of Cairo was the same as when the Carruths were there last time. The merchants on the streets were still selling their wares, and the beautiful museum still looked as magnificent as ever. As everyone climbed out of the SUV and headed into the Museum, Tyler noticed the same Bentley he'd seen at the airport. "Hey, Mom, who do we know that would be riding in a Bentley?"

"I don't know of anyone . . . why?" Ellie asked as she grabbed her briefcase from the vehicle's front seat.

"Because I saw that Bentley over there at the airport," Tyler replied, pointing to the sleek black car waiting just around the corner from the museum.

"Son, that car at the airport probably wasn't the only Bentley in Cairo," Ellie explained.

"But it is. It's the same one. I recognize the driver," Tyler retorted.

"Okay, so they have business close by. Now, come on! We have things to do." Ellie grabbed Tyler's backpack by the straps and began to pull him into the Museum doorway. Tyler strained to stretch his neck back for another glimpse. There was something about that car and that driver that was vaguely familiar.

"Mom, I'm going with Naeem and Ahmal. Okay?"

"That's fine, but hurry back," Ellie replied.

"Naeem! Wait up!" Tyler quickly ran to catch up to Naeem and Ahmal. The three veered off and headed to the back of the museum towards Ahmal's office.

Suzi, her mom, and Emma headed down the long marble hallway to the museum's executive offices. Just then, a tall, dark man with tousled hair, wearing a relaxed gray suit, stepped out of the office and headed in their direction.

"Papa!" exclaimed Emma.

"Emma! Ohhh, I have missed you so much." He grabbed her up and hugged her tightly, kissing her on the forehead. "Let me look at you!" Instantly, Asim stopped, held her by the shoulders, and asked, "Emma! Is that makeup you are wearing?"

"Do you like it? Aunt Annah bought it for me." Emma continued, "She has a friend who is a Las Vegas showgirl. She gave me makeup lessons! Isn't it wonderful?" She once again kissed her father on the cheek, leaving him stunned. She walked past him and toward the door of his office. She stopped just shy of the doorway, glanced back at Suzi and Ellie, and gave them a quick wink.

Suzi and Ellie giggled to themselves as they followed a speechless Dr. Nasar into his office, the Office of Excavation and Research. "Okay, that was just wrong," Suzi snickered.

After pulling himself together, Asim turned to Ellie. "Hello, Dr. Carruth. It is nice to finally meet you in person. I am Asim Nasar. We spoke on the phone a few weeks ago."

"Yes, Asim. It's my pleasure. Please call me Ellie," she replied. Reaching to shake his hand, she continued. "You know, I was thinking after we spoke on the phone, my husband mentioned someone named *Asim Nasar* several times when he'd take on projects near the western part of Egypt and in Libya near Tripoli. You wouldn't happen to be *that Asim*, would you?"

"Yes, madam. I knew your husband well," Asim replied with a smile. "I was a brand new Archaeologist with our team when he was the Chief Archaeologist. He taught me a great deal, and I was very grateful for his tutelage. Jason was a good man and an even better friend. I was very sorry to hear of his passing."

"Thank you, that's very kind. Well, if you are as good now as Jason said you were back then, then we're in very good hands!" Ellie replied.

Dr. Nasar nodded and smiled gratefully. "Please, have a seat!"

Nasar's office was enormous. In addition to the seemingly endless shelves of books, there were three tables with artifacts, parchments, and notebooks scattered everywhere. In the corner sat Nasar's small but beautifully carved desk made from Sycamore wood. Near the desk were two exquisite chairs that appeared to be from the 17th or 19th dynasty of Egyptian royalty.

Immediately, Suzi went straight for the chairs to inspect them. She stroked the angles and touched the seats, not missing a single artistic detail. Her eyes wide and in sheer awe, she asked, "Are these real?"

Nasar then chuckled and replied, "Oh no, dear. I have a very close friend who deals in, what you would call them? Fakes. I want people to be able to sit in them."

Suzi continued to stare at the chairs, amazed at the craftsmanship. "Fakes? Woah! These are fantastic!"

"Why, thank you." Nasar looked at Ellie. "She has her father's eye for details."

"She does . . . but I think it's more her grandfather in her. He could spot art a mile away."

Emma walked over and sat in a beautiful gold and ebony chair that had been carefully placed next to her father's desk. "This is my favorite."

"Mine too," Nasar said with a nostalgic smile.

Emma looked at Suzi. "It was a gift from my Mum."

Nasar kissed his daughter on the top of her head, looked at her, and said, "Yes, it was." He then clasped his hands together, leaned against the corner of his desk, and said, "Okay, well, I am sure everyone would like to have dinner and turn in early tonight before we begin our preparations early tomorrow morning."

"That sounds great, but have you heard from Mandi Menkura?" Ellie asked Nasar. "We usually review the project details while traveling together on the plane, but she didn't fly with us this time. She said she'd meet us here. I still haven't heard from her."

"Yes, actually. She was here but left just moments before

you arrived." Nasar continued, "She mentioned that she had planned to meet you all later."

Ellie quickly looked at her cell phone. No calls. This was not like her friend. "If you hear from her again, please ask her to call me," Ellie continued. "I need to chat with her soon!"

Nasar replied, "Yes, certainly."

Tyler ran up to meet them just as they headed out the office door into the hallway. "Hey, Mom, can we get something to eat? I'm getting hungry."

"You're always hungry," Suzi quipped.

"I'm growing!" Tyler replied.

"Uh-huh, you're growing alright." Suzi poked at her brother's belly.

"Hey! I am not fat!" Tyler growled and swatted Suzi's hand away. "I'm *athletic*!" Tyler was in excellent shape. Although he loved junk food, he was active enough in sports to stay fairly fit. However, it was one of Suzi's favorite ways to tease him.

"Come on, you two. Give it a rest," Ellie scolded. The back-and-forth between them was exhausting. It had been a long day, and they were all tired and hungry. Food was definitely next on the agenda. "Let's go find some dinner," Ellie said.

Emma laughed at the Carruth siblings and looked up at her father. "I want a brother or sister!"

To which her father stared at her and replied, "First makeup, and now a sibling? You are never going to America again! Is that clear?"

Emma smiled sweetly, "If you say so, Papa." She placed her arm around her father's waist. She was so happy to be home and missed her father very much. After her mother died, her father was left to care for her by himself. But now that Emma was older, it was a toss-up as to who was actually caring for whom. Emma really bucked her father's decision to send her to America while he settled into his new position. She simply was not accustomed to being so far away from him for so long. None of that mattered now. She was home and had absolutely no plans to go back to Las Vegas ever again.

Asim and Emma followed the Carruths out of the museum to the car that had been waiting for them just outside. Everyone agreed on a time to meet the next morning to get their project underway. Emma and her dad had just turned to walk back into the building when Nasar's cell phone rang. He answered and said, "She is waiting for your call." After a short pause, "I understand, but you must call her soon. She will become suspicious." Then Nasar hung up his phone and opened the museum door to let Emma walk in ahead of him. Emma entered the door and asked, "Who was that, Papa?"

"No one, my dear. Now come here, and tell me all about America and this 'Las Vegas.' How are your uncle and my sister?"

7

The Egyptian desert can reach over one hundred degrees during the day in June. During the summer months, water was nearly as valuable as gold, so when packing for these trips, water containers, food rations, and supplies took up a lot of space in the vehicles. There were also many crew members on the team, and as a result, each member must bring specific equipment and supplies they needed to perform their jobs and a few personal belongings.

Packing began before dawn, and everyone had to contribute to ensuring the team left Cairo with enough time to reach the dig site well before sunset.

Ellie loaded her brushes and tools onto the Jeep, then noticed her son sitting in the front seat, fooling around with his cell phone. "Ty, please go over to the storeroom and help Ahmal get food and supplies together." However, Tyler, still concentrating on his cell phone, ignored his mother's request. "Ty, son, did you hear me?"

"Okay, Mom, just a second. I'm trying to get a Wi-Fi connection." Tyler was moving his phone around in various directions, trying to get a signal, when he noticed the angry and stressed glare from his mother. He quickly decided it would be in his best interest to do as he was told.

Watching Ellie handle her son, Asim walked up and laughed. "I remember when he was born."

Ellie looked at Asim. "Really?"

"If you will remember, Jason came to Tripoli shortly after his son's birth. He must have shown me fifty photographs of his new son. He was a very proud papa."

Ellie smiled. "He was that way after both of the kids were born. He adored them."

Asim placed his hand on Ellie's shoulder. "He was a good man."

"Yes. Yes, he was." Ellie quickly pulled herself together from the sting of being back in Egypt after her husband's death. She grabbed a few maps and documents from the jeep's front seat. "Okay, so my information and research, along with your sources, places our focus in this area . . . here . . . to the south." Ellie pointed to a region in the southern area of the Valley of the Queens. Asim and Ellie stood next to the Jeep with maps spread across the hood and continued discussing the project's final maps, plans, and trip documents.

"Did Dr. Menkura contact you last evening?" Asim asked Ellie.

"Yes, finally. We spoke very briefly last night. I was beginning to wonder if she was going to make it today. But she assured me she'd be out here bright and early this morning. Hopefully, she'll get here soon," Ellie replied as she scanned the area.

"I am sure she will do as promised, Dr. Carruth," Nasar commented.

"Ellie, please. I'm just Ellie," she said as she lifted another box of parchment rolls and maps onto the Jeep hood. "Of course, ma'am. Ellie," Nasar replied with a smile. "Let me take these to the storeroom for you. I assume these will not be needed."

"Thanks, Asim. Everything in here is too outdated for us to use."

As Asim was walking away, Suzi and Emma approached, dragging an empty box that once had supplies in it. "Mom, the rest of the tools are loaded onto the truck. Nora said to tell you she's going back to the Museum to see if Jake has shown up yet. His plane was running late. I hope he makes it!"

No sooner had Suzi finished her statement than a voice came from behind her. "Now you know I would never miss a chance to hang out with my favorite aunt and cousins for the summer."

"Jake!" Suzi exclaimed as she jumped and gave her cousin a big hug. She then turned to introduce him to her new friend. "Jake, this is Emma . . . Emma, Jake. He's our mapper . . . and our cousin. He works closely with Mom and the rest of the team to document where the artifacts are found and where we dig next based on data." Since this was Emma's first time doing an archaeological digging project, Suzi took it upon herself to explain things as they went along.

Ellie set the tool pouch she was holding on the ground to hug her nephew properly. "Jake! Oh, it is so good to see you! How are you? And how is that overworked brother of mine?"

"I'm good, Auntie. So is he . . . the doctor put him on anxiety medications, and Mom's sitting on him to take them like he is supposed to," Jake said as he kissed his aunt on the cheek. "They both send their love."

"Well, next time you talk to him, tell him he does not want his baby sister dropping international projects to come to New York to pull him off that stock exchange floor!" Ellie pointed a finger and winked.

"I will," Jake smiled. "I'm sure Mom could use the backup when it comes to Dad's stubbornness." Jake surveyed the ongoing packing. "I see you have things fully under control as usual."

"Well, it's coming together," Ellie looked around with her hands on her hips.

"Hey, Mom. I am going to tell Nora that Jake is here. Okay?"

"Okay, Suz, thanks. And could you also go over and help Ahmal straighten out the boys?" Ellie continued, "Playing football with the food packages is not getting it loaded up."

"Nooo problem!" Suzi agreed as she and Emma left to find Nora, then head over to the storeroom to put the boys back in line.

"Good ole' Suzi the Enforcer," Jake laughed, as he grabbed his knapsack. "You know, a few questionable individuals in Manhattan could use an *enforcer* like her," he joked. Ellie snickered as she raised her eyebrows and nodded in agreement.

"Did Nora keep her same team of diggers this year?" Jake asked as they walked together toward a stack of boxes. "She threatened to fire everyone last time for laughing when Tyler put that fake snake in her bunk."

"Yeah, most of them have returned." Ellie snickered and then noticed Asim Nasar returning from the storeroom.

"Oh, Jake. This is Asim . . . " Ellie began.

Jake interrupted with a big grin, "Right! Nasar. Hey man, how've you been?"

"I have been well, Carter. And you?" Asim replied with a giant handshake and bear hug.

Ellie chimed in. "Wait, you two know one another?"

"Yeah, of course. We worked with Uncle Jason a couple of times back when I was a new intern in college. Asim here was a green Archaeologist. Plus, I just saw you . . . when was it? In November?" Jake recalled, then continued, "How's that little girl of yours?"

"Yes, I believe that was at the National Geographic Conference in London," Asim replied with a smile. "And Emma isn't so 'little' anymore. She came home from America wearing makeup!"

"I think that just happens, man," Jake laughed and patted his friend on the shoulder.

Ellie was surprised but happy. "I guess it only makes sense you two would have worked together with Jason at some point. Okay! This is excellent!"

Asim was excited to see someone he knew and trusted. They had been good friends and worked well together back in the day.

"Well, I have some work to finish inside the museum. We will catch up later, Jake!" Asim shook his friend's hand again and headed towards the museum.

"Definitely!" Jake replied.

Ellie and her nephew collected the leftover boxes and bags and walked off towards the storeroom, discussing his latest trip to Nepal. Jake was only twenty-eight years old but one of the most sought-after mapping experts in the world. It did not matter how busy he was; he would always set aside time to work with his favorite aunt on whatever project she had going on. He loved his aunt dearly and understood the importance of her work. Not to mention the fact she, too, was highly sought after in the archaeological world. In many ways, he connected with his aunt better than with his parents. His father, Ellie's older brother, Ian, was a Stockbroker on Wall Street. His mother, Maggie, who'd been raised on a farm in rural Virginia, had taken to the big city life very well as a NY Stockbroker's wife. On the other hand, Jake was born with the same traveling genes as his aunt. For years, Jake and his father were at odds over Jake's choice of career. He wanted Jake to become a doctor or a lawyer. But one day, Ian read an article in the *New York*

Times about a rising young star in the archaeological world. As he read, he realized his son was the focus of this amazing article. He read about his son's unbelievable accomplishments and realized this was what he was meant to do. At this time, he gave his son complete support and encouragement, with a few parental warnings that he should be careful.

Jake sat his boxes down at the storeroom door, hugged his aunt again, and headed over to the museum to finalize his maps for the trek into the desert. After taking everything inside, Ellie began to walk back toward the supply tent, carrying a few notebooks and supplies, when a Bentley pulled up behind her. Ellie turned to look and out popped her old college friend and colleague, Mandi. "Ell!" Mandi exclaimed as she hugged her old friend.

"Hello, stranger!" Ellie replied.

"You look great! How have you been?" Mandi asked.

"Aw, thanks! I'm okay. We are managing. Jason's death took its toll on us for a while. The kids took it really hard. But we're doing alright. I'm looking forward to getting back into things again." Ellie continued, "We took the summer off last year."

"Probably a good idea. I follow the kids on social media. Suzi seems to be excited to be here."

"That's an understatement. She was beyond bored last year," Ellie commented. "Sad and bored makes for a grumpy teenager."

"Oh, I bet!" Mandi paused, "I'm sorry I wasn't able to chat much last night. My father had me busy working on things for him."

"Your father is *here*?"

"Yeah, he's at the hotel in the city center."

"Oookay," Ellie said with a bit of confusion. "Is he planning to join us?" she continued with a wink.

Mandi laughed. "Girl, if he weren't too old, you know he'd be right out there with us tomorrow. But no, he's here on business, which is why I couldn't meet you guys in London. He needed me to travel with him. We had some things to discuss."

"Oh, okay. I see. That makes sense. Well, you're here now, so let's get started. Walk with me to the storeroom while I fill you in on some things," Ellie replied. But before they could walk away, Suzi came running up from behind.

"Aunt Mandi!" Suzi exclaimed.

"Doodle! How is my goddaughter?" Mandi hugged Suzi tightly. "I have missed you so much!"

"I'm good! Why didn't you fly in with us yesterday?" Suzi asked.

"My father and I had business, and we needed to tend to it yesterday," Mandi replied.

"Gotcha!" Suzi continued. "I'm glad you made it." Suzi smiled and gave her godmother another huge hug.

"Suz, go finish loading the last of the supplies. We need to be packed and ready to go by ten a.m.," Ellie instructed.

"Okay. See you later, Aunt Mandi." Off Suzi went to finish loading the trucks.

"She has gotten so grown up!" Mandi said as she took several of the notebooks from Ellie.

"Yep, and even more *Suzi-like*," Ellie laughed.

"Uh oh . . . " Mandi replied as the two old friends laughed and walked to the building, chatting away about the project and what they could expect to find in the Valley of the Queens. Mandi and Ellie had been friends since their college days at Oxford University in England. Because they had been such close friends, Suzi and Ty called Mandisa "Aunt Mandi," even though they were not really related.

The project crew consisted of many different people, all of whom had specific jobs. Even the children had jobs and responsibilities.

As Chief Archaeologist, Ellie did all the very delicate digging, brushing, and scraping to uncover fragile items exposed by the digging crew. It was also her job to help correctly identify the artifacts they uncovered. Ellie had worked with this outstanding crew many times before, all except Dr. Nasar.

Dr. Asim Nasar was recently appointed to his post as Director of Excavation, and he replaced the retired Dr. Yashi Coulier. Dr. Nasar's job was overseeing the excavation and ensuring all the Egyptian government's protocols were followed. He also represented the museum's interests in Cairo and cared for all items recovered from the dig. Ellie was a bit relieved when this change took place. She felt Dr. Coulier didn't always have the museum's best interests in mind. Nothing she could explain, but there were occasions when Dr. Coulier chose a path that did not reflect well on the museum but financially benefited Coulier himself. None of that mattered anymore. The museum had a new Director of Excavation and Research. And he came highly recommended by none other than her late husband. This alone made Ellie smile because it was almost as if Jason was watching over them.

French and Egyptian, Nora Mansour was the Crew Chief. She managed a top-notch digging crew of Egyptian men. The digging crew did all the heavy lifting and digging, which allowed the archaeologists to get in to do the finer scraping and brushing.

Ahmal Patier, born and raised in Egypt, had been the Chief Excavator on all of Dr. Carruth's Egyptian and Middle Eastern digs for nearly twenty years. He had also accompanied Ellie and Jason on treks in Greece, Turkey, and several prehistoric sites in central Africa. Ahmal was whom the digging crew and their chief, Nora, reported to. He was responsible for all supplies, the workers, and their equipment, and made sure they stayed on schedule.

The project mapper, Jake Carter, provided the team with a working map to get them to and from their digging sites. He also documented and updated maps as new tombs, monuments, and artifacts were found.

The team's Egyptologist was Dr. Mandisa Menkura, whose job was to work closely with the archaeologist to label and identify all items the team uncovered correctly. Although Mandisa's mother was English, her father was Moroccan and Egyptian, which influenced Mandi's life and career. Ellie and Mandisa always worked very well together as a team.

Suzi and Tyler had specific jobs on the team as well. One of Suzi's many jobs was to help catalog artifacts. It was not the most exciting job, but she didn't mind helping. Suzi had more of a delicate touch and could assist her mother with the finer brushing and digging. Ty was not as skilled with brushes, so he did manual work with Naeem and his father, Ahmal. On occasion, Tyler was invited to help his cousin, Jake, survey and map the area. He enjoyed this very much. Mapping was to Tyler, as the detailed excavation was to his sister . . . everything.

8

The Valley of the Queens
near Luxor, Egypt

Located just south of the Valley of the Kings, on the west bank of the Nile River, and across from the modern city of Luxor, rested the Valley of the Queens. The trek down was long and hot. Not only was the heat a problem, but the jeeps and trucks offered an extremely bumpy ride, which made comfort nonexistent. The drive took hours, and by the time they finally arrived in the valley, it had been an exceptionally long day, and everyone was exhausted.

With only an hour or so of daylight left, they quickly found the location of their excavation site and set up camp. Every crew member had a job, and the chores of setting up base camp went like clockwork. Once the work tents were set up, dinner was prepared. Everyone had worked hard, and food was a welcomed sight. Tyler did not care much for Egyptian cuisine, but even he stuffed himself full. Once dinner had been eaten and clean up was complete, the crew began putting up the sleeping tents. Tomorrow would be a busy day, and an early bedtime was in order. Suzi, Tyler, Naeem, and their new friend Emma were completely exhausted and didn't make much of a fuss when told to go to their tents for the night. Suzi's thoughts raced, however, as she eyed the newly set up research tent across the camp.

"Ty, you go on. I need to check on something. I'll be there

in a few minutes," Suzi motioned to her brother as she turned to walk away.

Tyler looked at his sister with the usual suspicion. "Okay, but you know you can't be out here too late," he warned.

"Yeah, yeah, I know. I'll hurry," Suzi scoffed.

He shook his head, gave her one more cautious look, then went off to bed. Suzi walked in the direction of the research tent. Upon arrival, she looked around to see if anyone was looking, then slipped quickly inside. She pulled a small flashlight out of her pocket and looked over the maps and documents left on the tables. She reviewed each piece of information, each clue, and each map. She took out her cell phone and snapped a few photographs of documents she wanted to look at later, as well as Jake's initial map of the dig site. Suddenly, she heard her mother and Mandi approaching the tent. She frantically looked around. She needed an exit and fast! Her mother would be upset if she caught her here without permission. She crawled under the back flap just in the nick of time.

"Whew! That was close," a voice said from behind her. Suzi jumped and caught her breath as she realized it was Emma.

"What are you doing here?" Suzi hissed as her heart raced.

"I could ask you the same thing," Emma whispered in return.

Suzi stood up, took a deep breath, and relaxed. She grabbed Emma's jacket and pulled her well out of earshot of the research tent. "I was looking at my mom's notes, okay?"

"Why?" Emma asked.

"Shhhhh!" Suzi pulled her even farther away. "Do you want us to get caught?"

Emma giggled. "You mean *you* get caught."

Still using a whisper, "Yeah, okay … me."

"So, what's up?" Emma quietly asked. "Why were you

snooping?"

"I wasn't snoop . . . okay yeah, I was snooping, but I always snoop," Suzi continued and looked around to make sure they were alone. "It's how I learn things. Mom doesn't take the time to tell me until later."

"But, why snoop? Why don't you just ask?" Emma thought it was just common sense.

"Because … she says I ask way too many questions." Suzi continued to look around.

"Do you?" Emma returned outside of a whisper.

"Shhhh! Yes, of course, I do."

"Well, there you have it," Emma shrugged her shoulders.

"I can't help it. I get curious. I have to know," Suzi admitted.

Emma stared at Suzi for a minute and said, "Ooookay. Well, we should get back before *we* get caught." Suzi smiled at her new friend, and then the two of them tiptoed back to the sleeping tents.

As the sun peeked across the horizon of the Egyptian desert little by little, the crew began to stir, and the camp came to life. The excitement of a new dig filled the air. Suzi was in her element. Every year, just after Christmas, she counted the weeks until it was time to leave on these summer trips. She loved this stuff! This was what she wanted to do when she grew up. She wanted to go to Oxford University and become an archaeologist, which surprised absolutely no one. Both of her parents and her grandfather were all archaeologists and Oxford University graduates. She had been tagging along with them on these trips every year since she was very young. Suzi took to archaeology naturally and quickly. Her aptitude for this science was as natural as learning to walk. Tyler, on the other hand, was not as keen on becoming an archaeologist as his sister. He loved sports and wanted to be a professional hockey player when he grew up. After all, he led his league in goals every winter. Tyler enjoyed these trips with his family but missed the friends he left behind in the summertime. Although his friends thought trekking across the world was *totally cool*, he looked forward to the fall to get back to hockey and hang out with his buddies.

The crew set up their stations and worked to find where to begin their search. As Suzi began getting dressed, thoughts of the day ahead consumed her. She could think of nothing else as she reviewed all the evidence in her head. She thought back to her mother's notes she'd read while waiting at the London airport. The notes, the maps, and the documents in the research tent from other scientists. *Could it be?* Suzi thought to herself. She could not wait. She had to tell Naeem and Emma, and yeah, okay, Tyler, too.

She scurried over to the mess tent to find the others, and her mind continued to ramble. "Those scientists . . . They were all looking for Queen Nefertiti's tomb," Suzi thought out loud. "But no real evidence has ever been found . . . there has always been a great deal of talk about where she 'might' be buried . . . but nothing . . . Okay, scientists and Egyptologists have studied evidence about her, but again, nothing . . . they've found nothing . . . Well, nothing that could be proven anyway. The KV34 tomb is in the Valley of the Kings, and even Amarna itself, but there is no concrete evidence of her. They've found mummies they thought could be her but found out later it was someone else."

"Are you talking to yourself?" Nora suddenly appeared and asked Suzi.

"Oh! Umm, no . . . " Startled, Suzi replied, embarrassed,

then continued on her way.

Perplexed, Nora watched Suzi as she walked towards the mess tent, "Wait. How'd you know? Oh, never mind. One of these days, you are going to find yourself in a whole lot of trouble, lil' miss," Nora mumbled to herself as she continued off toward the toilet, magazine in hand.

Suzi crept around to the side of the mess tent, trying to get the others' attention without drawing too much attention to herself. "Psssst. Pssst!" hissed Suzi. "Hey! You guys! Get over here!"

Confused, they looked at Suzi as if she were crazy. "Okay, this better be good, Suz. I am starving!" complained Tyler as he rolled his eyes. The three of them strolled over to her, breakfast in hand.

"Yeah, well, you're always starving," Suzi returned. "But listen. I know where we are going."

"What do you mean? We are already here," Emma asked.

"She means she knows what the team is here to look for," Naeem smiled. "You know, don't you?"

With a mischievous wink, Suzi replied, "Yep!"

With a mouthful of cereal, Tyler chimed in, "Did Mom tell you? Mom never tells me anything," as he dropped his spoon into a half-full bowl of milk.

Wiping the splattered cereal milk from her clothes, Suzi sighed and proceeded to tell them all about how she figured it out. Emma caught Suzi's eye with a raised eyebrow and a smirk, but Suzi pretended not to notice.

"Well, to start with, I overheard Mom and Naeem's dad on the phone a few days after Dr. Nasar called. Mom slipped up once and referred to her as *the Queen*. It got me thinking. So, I pulled some of Mom's recent notes from the computer and started reading about the 18th Dynasty and the lack of evidence surrounding Akhenaten, his family, and his reign." Suzi continued, "Once at the airport, I took the opportunity to look through Mom's notes again while you two were sleeping. The notes mentioned 'the queen who seemed to have just disappeared.' They also mentioned something about a compromised grave site."

"I can never read her writing. And I always get caught! How do you get away with this crap?" Tyler retorted.

"Um, I *do* get caught. A lot," Suzi said as a matter of fact, then continued, "So, when I ran across the maps and a few more documents in the research tent."

"Ran across?" Emma's sarcasm was difficult to ignore this time.

"Okay, okay, so I went looking . . . whatever." Suzi continued, "Anyway, it confirms that they may have hard evidence that Queen Nefertiti is somewhere near here!"

Tyler asked, "What kind of *hard evidence*?"

"Something about a theft from a tomb nearby. Apparently, the black market has been frantically looking for some artifact."

"The black market? Suzi, that is dangerous." Naeem was concerned.

"Ehh, it'll be fine! That's probably going on somewhere in Europe anyway. They aren't likely to be here. They don't even know we're here. This dig has been kept quiet," Suzi replied, trying to ease her friend's mind. "Now . . . what's for breakfast?" Suzi rubbed her hands together. "Smells delicious!"

The kids returned to their table. They agreed that this was no ordinary dig. Their team was there to look for one of the most elusive Egyptian queens in history.

9

The excitement of the week ahead was evident throughout camp. The crew started work right away. They laid outlines and plans based on Jake's maps. The kids, too, had plans, and even though all four of them had jobs and responsibilities, they still enjoyed a great deal of free time in the afternoons. Generally, the afternoons in the desert were too hot; therefore, most of the hard digging and sifting was done before 1:00 p.m. With this in mind, they sought to figure out when all four would be free, at the same time. Their goal was to set out on their own to investigate the surrounding caves. Suzi was scheduled to help her mother and Mandi most of the morning, while Emma assisted her dad, whose job was to review documents and sort through maps with Jake. Tyler and Naeem would be with the diggers, retrieving digging utensils and equipment. As basic as this sounds, it was an extremely helpful job. It saved the digging crew a great deal of time. Not to mention, Tyler and Naeem kept the crew very amused with their practical jokes and pranks. The time the two of them put a rubber cobra in Nora's knapsack was very vivid in the minds of the crew. The digging crew had an enormous amount of respect for Nora, but seeing their Crew Chief streak across the desert half-naked and screaming was one of their most memorable moments. They laughed for hours, and although Tyler and Naeem were, in fact, heroes in the eyes of the crew, they were in big trouble with their parents. Not to mention the berating they got from Nora once she calmed down. But knowing how much amusement they gave the entire crew made the punishment somewhat bearable. Oh, who were they kidding? It was totally worth it!

As the four of them finished their breakfast, they huddled in the corner of the mess tent, trying not to draw attention to themselves.

"Okay, everyone, listen," Naeem leaned in. "My cousin, Tarik, works in the documents and map room at the museum. He said there were a couple of caves the museum investigated as possible digging sites."

"Excellent. Do you know where they are exactly?" Suzi asked.

"Yes, I believe so," Naeem responded.

"You *believe* so?" Emma quickly reacted. This was Emma's first time out, and getting lost was not an option.

"Yes, yes, I know where they are. Sheesh. I came out here with my father to look over the early maps Jake FedExed last month," Naeem defended.

"I trust you, Naeem," encouraged Suzi as she patted him on the shoulder.

"Me too," agreed Tyler.

Still a little hesitant, Emma shook her head in agreement. "Oh, alright."

The time had been set. The four of them decided to meet behind the equipment tent at 2 p.m. It was the first day of the dig, and they all had very busy mornings.

"Good! I'll be able to eat lunch before we head out," Tyler remarked.

"Okay, let's all set our watches," Naeem whispered.

Digital watches beeped; they quickly split up and went about their assigned duties.

As the morning went on, Suzi found it increasingly difficult to concentrate on her work. She could not wait till the 1 o'clock lunch break. She felt like her stomach was turning inside out.

An artifacts table had been set up just outside the research tent to place any items found during excavation. Mandi and Ellie were to oversee this station, and Suzi was there to help. However, just as Ellie feared, Suzi would be full of questions. She wanted to know what exactly they thought they'd find on this expedition.

"So, Mom, where do you expect to find Nefertiti?" Suzi casually asked, as if she had been involved in the planning of this project from the onset, but she was a little startled when Mandi suddenly dropped a box of digging utensils.

Ellie leaned forward onto the table she was working on and sighed. Then, shaking her head, she bent down to help Mandi clean up the scattered array of digging tools and brushes.

"How long have you known?" Ellie asked as she picked up the utensils. She was not the least bit surprised. Irritated, yes, but not surprised.

It wasn't the fact Suzi knew what they were looking for that irritated her so much, as it was Suzi's insistence that her mother's work was open for her review any time she wanted. "Never mind, don't answer that. Young lady, you and I really need to have another discussion about boundaries and snooping into my files."

"What snooping? I was just reading." Suzi tried to defer her mother's frustrations with sarcasm, but it didn't work. Ellie looked up from the mess on the ground and simply glared at her daughter.

"Suzanna, there are notes in those files that are not for just anyone to see," Ellie continued. "The Egyptian government is not in the business of providing amusement for precocious fourteen-year-olds." Given her mother's unsettling calm demeanor, Suzi knew her mom was extremely irritated with her. It might be in her best interests to simply be quiet.

"Yes, ma'am," Suzi conceded.

Mandi took it all in and tried to decide if she should be worried about her goddaughter. Suzanna was indeed 'precocious,' and her love for this atmosphere could complicate Mandi's purpose on this project.

As the morning progressed, slowly and carefully, Suzi began to ask her mother and Aunt Mandi questions about the project and about Nefertiti herself. Ellie, being a patient mom, answered her daughter's questions as best as she could. She knew Suzi would never give up unless she did. Besides, as irritated as she was with her, she also loved the fact that her daughter was so interested in her work.

Suzi had read several books on Nefertiti in school and knew that little was known about her marriage to Akhenaton, the movement of Egypt's capital from Thebes to Amarna, and Nefertiti's reign as Queen. All this made Suzi even more excited to be there. She saw this afternoon's secret stroll to the outskirts of camp as her chance to investigate things for herself. Who knows, she might even be the person who finds Nefertiti herself.

After lunch, several crewmembers mingled around the mess tent before returning to their stations. Because of the desert heat, most of the afternoon was spent cleaning up from the morning's work. Soon, the subtle sound of four digital watches began to ring out at various locations around camp. One by one, the children appeared behind the equipment tent. Suzi and Tyler arrived first, with Emma next, followed closely by Naeem.

"Everyone ready?" Suzi whispered intently as if the mission they were undertaking was a matter of international security.

Shaking his head at her, Tyler simply said, "Yeah . . . " then whispered back to Naeem, "She takes this crap way too seriously."

Laughing, Naeem moved ahead of the others and motioned them to follow him. "This way, guys."

Suddenly, it dawned on Suzi. She remembered Naeem telling her he knew about a cave he wanted to explore before they left the States. She also remembered him saying that he came out here with his dad to review the site with Jake's maps. Suzi walked ahead to where Naeem was leading them out of base camp. As she reached him, she tugged on the back of his shirt and hissed, "You knew, didn't you?" Suzi continued. "You knew when you messaged me last spring that we were coming *here* to look for Nefertiti's tomb."

Naeem smiled really big and looked at his friend. "I did, yes."

"Why didn't you tell me?"

"Because… uh, I wanted to surprise you!" He continued to mumble as he walked off. "That … and my father would have killed me if I had said anything."

Suzi just stood and looked at Naeem as he continued to walk towards an entrance to a cave. After the ripping she received from her mom earlier in the day, she kind of understood . . . but still! She stammered as she tried to speak and finally just mumbled and groaned to herself. Tyler walked past his *all-knowing* sister and snickered.

10

After a short five-minute walk across a short patch of flat desert, they approached a small band of hills and cliffs less than a quarter mile from camp. On a ledge about five feet off the ground was a hole nearly six feet wide. Though the size or depth of the cave was unclear, it was obviously a cave of some sort. The four of them shimmied up a few moderately sized boulders and climbed easily onto the entrance ledge.

"In here!" Naeem exclaimed as he walked into the entrance of the cave.

"Uh, dude, it's really dark in there!" responded Tyler nervously.

Emma reached down and grabbed the flashlight hanging on Tyler's belt. "Here, don't be such a wimp."

"Hey!" Ty said with as much *man tone* as he could muster. "I'm not a wimp!"

Walking up behind Tyler, Suzi gave him a quick poke. "Boo!"

Tyler jumped. "Agh!"

"Right," Suzi hissed as she walked past her brother.

"Very funny. Wait up." Tyler hurried to catch up with the others.

The four of them walked straight through the dark and damp cavern for a while before they approached a perpendicular hallway. Having all four flashlights lit gave them a clear view of the walls surrounding them. The connecting wall that faced them was covered with a lot of hieroglyphics. They were simple, really: animals, the Nile, the sun, and basic Egyptian life. They were encouraging and inviting.

The four of them stood for a moment with their flashlights focused on the artwork. "This is beautiful," Emma commented.

"Yes, it is," Suzi replied with awe and wonder.

"I do not think it actually *says* anything, though," Naeem remarked.

"I don't either," Emma agreed.

"But it sure is pretty!" Suzi admired the wall from top to bottom and from side to side.

"Definitely," Emma agreed again.

"Okay, now where?" asked Tyler as he flipped his flashlight right at Naeem's face.

"How should I know? I've never been inside here before," Naeem responded. "And get that thing out of my face."

"Oh, sorry!" Tyler apologized and dropped the beam of his flashlight down to the floor.

"Did you bring a map?" Emma asked Naeem.

"Umm, nooo. My father never left one lying around for me to grab," Naeem replied, frustrated.

Emma stared at him in obvious disbelief, sighed, and replied, "Okay, well, let's see. Hoping my sense of direction is correct; if we go to the left, we will go toward the inside of the mountain. If we go to the right, we will head to the cave's edge." Emma paused. "Wait a minute. Look at these hieroglyphs again . . . but closer." She stared at the drawings. "These animals and people . . . they all seem to be looking in this direction," Emma pointed. "To the left, towards the inside of the cave."

"To the left, it is then," Suzi responded immediately. "It's almost as if we're being invited in." She turned left to walk in the direction the pictures pointed.

The others followed Suzi's lead down the corridor. The walls of the cave seemed to almost close in on them a little; the hallway seemed to become narrower as they walked. With their flashlights guiding their way, the corridor felt darker and colder than before. It wasn't long before Suzi noticed a strange smell. One Suzi recognized right away.

"Ty, do you smell Grampa?" she asked.

"Huh?" Ty replied.

Suzi stopped, grabbed her brother's shirt, and hissed, "I said, do you smell Grampa?"

Realizing right away what she was talking about, Tyler quickly responded. "Woah, wait, I do!"

Emma and Naeem both looked at the other two curiously. "What are you two talking about?" Emma finally asked.

"Shh! Did you hear that?" Suzi exclaimed.

"Hear what?" the other three responded all at once.

"Shhhhh!" Suzi insisted, frozen in her steps, as she silenced the others.

Fearing a punch from his sister, Ty stepped out of striking distance and whispered, "I don't hear anything."

Suzi looked at him, pressed her finger to her lips to be quiet, and then put her hand out in front of herself to signal the others to hold on and stand still. Suddenly, a noise came from behind them. Before the girls knew what was happening, both boys had jumped behind them.

Emma just shook her head. "Oh, please."

The smell began to get stronger, and even Naeem and Emma noticed the strange, spicy, sweet smell of clover and balsa wood. Fearing the steps were getting closer, Tyler looked back and then again at his sister. He nodded for her to keep going, and Suzi began to move on.

Emma grabbed Naeem by the front of his shirt and pulled their frightened friend along. "If I die in here, Papa is going to kill me," Naeem whimpered.

"Shhhh!" the other three hissed.

Tyler followed closely behind Naeem to keep him moving along. As the kids made their way through the cave, so did the smell, which unnerved Suzi. "Grampa died with Dad a year ago. How are we smelling Grampa's cologne?" she asked.

Suzi and Tyler looked at one another. They were very close to their grandfather and remembered the story he told them once about an old colleague who brought him a bottle of cologne from Japan. Grampa Carruth's actual profession was never really clear, but they knew their grandfather had many friends in many parts of the world. In his younger years, he had been an archaeologist, but later in life, he became somewhat of an "international businessman" who dealt with antiques and artifacts. Either way, his business dealings took him to some of ancient civilizations' oldest and most remote corners. Their parents had a good relationship with their grandfather, although Suzi could remember a few times when there had been conflict due to the nature of Grampa's "business." As Suzi grew older, she began to realize her grandfather was more of a treasure seeker and dealer in his later years rather than the scientist he once was. On occasion, when Collin Carruth worked on projects with his son and daughter-in-law, conflicts would sometimes occur regarding what to do with their findings. However, both parties eventually came to an understanding. More often than not, the items ended up in a museum.

Sadly, Suzi and Tyler lost both their father and their grandfather in a plane crash over the rainforest of Peru. But the children never forgot the spicy, sweet smell of their grandfather's Asian cologne; it was one of their most vivid memories. Strangely, they last smelled it when they hugged their grandfather goodbye the last time he visited. The fact that this smell was so strong was very unsettling for the Carruth children.

"Is it me, or is that smell getting stronger and those footsteps closer?" Naeem whispered.

At that moment, Suzi and Emma noticed a deep nook in the stone wall big enough for the kids to hide in. Emma motioned for the others to tuck in and hide. The kids huddled in the darkest corner of the nook and waited. It was only a matter of minutes before the pungent smell of sweat and cologne was upon them, and a dark shadow emerged against the cave wall. As they heard the heavy footsteps shuffling outside their hiding place, the four of them remained completely still. They held their breath as a strange man appeared. They could see him, but because of the shadows, he could not see them. The man was older and heavyset, wearing a tan linen suit and a crooked red bow tie. The temperature inside the cave was relatively cool, but the man's white shirt was stained and soaked from sweat. His round face was red and streaked as the sweat dripped from under his white hat. The man looked as if he had just stepped out of one of Grampa's old photographs, and Suzi was certain she'd seen him somewhere before. It bothered her that she could not think of why he was so familiar.

And why is he here? Suzi thought to herself. Confused, the man never noticed the nook right beside him. With his dim flashlight in hand, he continued down the narrow, dark hallway. The smell faded, but the kids continued to sit very still. They wanted to make absolutely sure the stranger had completely gone. The kids knew they had been followed. But why?

"Whew!" relaxed Naeem, as if he had held his breath the

entire time. "Who was that?"

"I don't know," Tyler waved his hand in front of his nose, "but he was disgusting! He smelled worse than Big Tom after a hockey game."

Emma responded, "Who's Big Tom?"

"Tom Morris, he plays hockey with me. Not a soul goes near him after a game; he sweats a ton, then drenches himself with cologne after the game. Sweat and cheap cologne . . . it's just nasty!" Tyler shuddered as he walked out of their hiding spot. "Ugghhh!"

Suzi chimed in, "Look, focus, you guys. I don't know who he is either, but we need to get out of here and head back to camp. I'm sure Mom's gonna be looking for us soon. Besides, I need to think."

Suzi walked cautiously toward the cave entrance, and the others quietly followed her.

The kids returned to camp just before dinner, only to find Aunt Mandi waiting for them at the edge of camp. "It's 4:00, and your parents are looking for you all."

"Umm, right, well, we uh, we were just looking at an old dig site close by and, uhhhh, just lost track of time," replied Tyler. The other three nodded so hard in agreement that one could almost hear their heads rattle. That story was as good as any at the moment. Suzi was actually quite impressed at his quick response.

They quickly walked past Aunt Mandi before she could question them further, but they knew her eyes were on their backs for quite some time. As soon as they had rounded the corner of the mess tent, they looked at each other as if they had just evaded the FBI.

11

The night sky fell upon the Egyptian desert. Outside the tents, the still breath of night was everywhere. Inside the tents, however, were many signs of life. Ellie, Mandi, Ahmal, and Jake were planning for tomorrow's work in the research tent. Several lanterns lit the large tent. Maps were spread out on tables with rocks holding down the corners so they could be read quickly. Ledger books were scattered across two tables for instant reference. A few artifacts had been located earlier in the day and were on the sifting table to be cleaned and analyzed further. Nora came into the tent carrying a small box containing soup, bread, and something to drink for each of them.

"What a day, huh?" Nora said as she stepped into the tent.

They all agreed, but as soon as they realized what she was carrying, they all sighed with great appreciation.

"Ahh! I'm starved!" Mandi acknowledged, and the others agreed.

"Thanks, Nora," Jake continued as he took a meal for himself. "I'll have these maps to your team first thing in the morning."

"Sounds good. See you all tomorrow. I'm turning in for the night," said Nora.

"Okay, good night," the rest of the group replied.

Nora left the tent and headed towards the sleeping tents near the back of the camp. Passing the Nasar's tent, Nora stopped by the door. "Knock, knock!" she said.

"Come in," Dr. Nasar replied as he looked up from the reports he had been working on.

Nora stuck her head in the doorway. "Hello, I just wanted to check in with Emma to see how she was getting along. I heard this was your first time out on one of these projects."

"I'm doing okay. Dad keeps me pretty busy," Emma responded, as Dr. Nasar gave a proud grin and a wink to Nora.

Nora looked at Emma and warned, "Look, you kids may want to stay closer to camp tomorrow, okay?" Nora smiled and added, "Goodnight! " before leaving and heading back to her sleeping tent.

"Night!" Emma and her dad replied.

Dr. Nasar's smile dropped, and he stared in disbelief at his daughter.

Emma's eyes widened as she fumbled in her knapsack, looking for a jacket to wear to dinner. "Oh, hey, it sure is getting cool out tonight. I should wear that pink jacket I brought."

Her dad was not going to let it go, however. "Seriously, Emma. First makeup, now sneaking off. What has gotten into you?"

"Okay, wait, Papa. The makeup thing . . . Well, that was just a *thing*. But today, we just went to the outskirts of the project area. I promise. We were *very* close by, and besides . . . Naeem knew exactly where we were." Which was a bit of a fib, and she knew it. But at least it eased her father's glare.

"Be careful out there, Emma! I would be devastated if anything happened to you. Now, go on and get some dinner. I will be down there once I finish documenting today's findings in the ledger."

"I will, Papa." Emma kissed her father on the cheek and headed out to meet her friends.

Neither Suzi nor Ty talked much during dinner. The day's events in the cave weighed on them heavily. It had only been a little over a year since they lost their father and grandfather, and the circumstances behind the plane crash were never made clear. The fact that this smelly stranger was in Egypt, at the very same location and at the very same time, was entirely too coincidental in Suzi's eyes. Suzi excused herself from dinner early. She wanted to go and think. It was strange really, but Suzi did her best thinking in the middle of nowhere. And the heart of the Egyptian desert, near the Valley of the Queens, was definitely nowhere.

It was about 7:30 p.m. when Tyler finally decided to leave the mess tent and talk to his sister. He knew they needed to chat about what happened in the cave earlier, but he thought it would be best just to give her time to sort it out for herself first. He caught Emma coming in just as he was leaving.

"Where is everyone?" Emma asked.

"Suzi didn't eat very much and left a while ago. Naeem ate quickly to help pull some tools for his dad and Jake for tomorrow. And I am heading out to find Suzi. I just thought she might want some dessert," Tyler explained as he held up a pie plate.

"Oh, okay, I'll catch up to everyone later. I'm starving," said Emma.

"Okay, see ya." Tyler smiled and left the mess tent. He walked two tents over to their sleeping tent, pulled the door flap back, and said, "Hey."

"Hey," Suzi looked up from below the bangs that had fallen from her lucky blue baseball cap. She wore that thing everywhere. At this point, however, it had failed to hold her long, wavy, brown hair. She was troubled, and it showed.

"I brought you some apple pie. There was a little leftover

from dinner. Nora made it, so I guess it's okay. I was kinda hoping Mom had made it, though."

"Thanks, but I'm not hungry," Suzi replied.

"Not even for pie?" Ty asked, but he knew the answer. His sister was tired and confused.

Ty placed the dish on the table and sat on the floor next to his sister. Together, they looked at the maps and notes Suzi had pulled out onto the floor. Suddenly, he realized these were different from the maps Jake had brought out earlier. These were old . . . *very old*. And the notes were in Dad's handwriting, not Mom's. "What's that you've got?" questioned Tyler.

"What does it look like?" his sister snapped back.

"Ooookay, well," Tyler stuttered.

"I'm sorry. I'm just frustrated. That man . . . why is he so familiar, Ty?"

Tyler crossed his legs and leaned in. "I think I have seen him before, and so have you, above Grampa's fireplace in one of those pictures," he said.

"Do you remember which one?" Suzi asked.

"Not sure off the top of my head, but I know that's where I have seen him before," Tyler answered.

Suzi sat straight up and said, "We must go back there. Tomorrow, we have to go back to the cave."

"It won't be easy to get away again, but I agree." Tyler relaxed and looked back down at the maps and papers scattered around his sister. "Okay, so, where'd you get all these?"

"I've had them for a long time. Dad gave them to me several years ago. Just thought it would be fun to have them along this time." A small tear dropped from her eye onto the map.

Tyler reached around Suzi's shoulder and gave her a little hug. "I miss him too, Suz."

A few minutes later, Naeem walked into the Carruth tent.

"Yikes, what is all this?" Naeem asked.

"Stuff from Dad's old files on Egypt. What's that you've got?" Tyler replied.

"A map I nicked from Dad's work tent," Naeem answered.

Both Tyler and Suzi's eyes lit up in amazement. "Nice! Aren't they going to know it's gone?" Tyler asked as he stood to examine the map his friend had 'borrowed.'

"They might, but I doubt it," Naeem continued, "This is the map Jake used to get started on the current one. They just tossed this one to the side. I picked it up like I was going to take it out with the trash."

"Ha! I love it!" exclaimed Suzi.

Suddenly, a dark shadow that formed at the back of their tent caught their attention. They all sat perfectly still, watching as the shadow moved across the back, around the side, and towards the front. Their eyes were wide open as Naeem found himself squarely perched behind Suzi. Suzi frowned and cut her eyes behind her.

"Seriously?" she hissed.

"What's that noise?" Naeem whispered.

"So, who's up for more pie?" Emma announced as she popped into the Carruth tent. All three kids exhaled as if they had not taken a breath in fifteen minutes. "Geez, Emma! You scared us to death," Tyler said.

"Ahh, not me. I knew it was you all along. These two were scared," Naeem commented, trying to shake it all off.

Suzi and Tyler quickly turned and stared at Naeem, who was still hiding behind Suzi.

"Um, yeah . . . well." Trying to recover, Naeem cleared his throat and sat next to Tyler.

Suzi stared at her for a moment and asked, "Emma? Where'd you get that hat?"

"Oh, this? I just picked it up outside the work tent. It's a bit smelly, really. I was going to give it to Nora. Thought it might belong to one of the workers."

"Emma, that is our *friend's* hat," responded Suzi.

"Huh? Friend? What friend?" Emma questioned.

"Look at it. It's the hat that old dude was wearing in the cave today," Suzi explained.

"Yuk! Oh nasty! Tell me you didn't put that stinky thing on your head!" exclaimed Tyler.

"Ugh! Gross! No way!" Emma shuddered, then quickly dropped the hat on the ground.

"Okay, we have bigger problems than whether or not Emma was wearing that hat," Suzi continued. "Why is it in our camp?"

"He's here? . . . with us? . . . in camp?" Naeem exclaimed. "I must tell my father right away!"

"Uh, *no*, you must *not* tell your father right away!" Suzi said boldly, with a bit of fear mixed in. "If we tell them, they will pack up and leave, and we will never know why he is here and why he seems so familiar. Not to mention, we will never find Nefertiti. So, no! We tell no one."

"I agree. I'm in!" Emma decided.

"Me too," Ty added.

The three of them looked at Naeem. "Yes, yes, okay. I am in, too. You crazy Americans are going to get me grounded again. I just know it."

"Excuse me? Aren't you the same kid *I heard* put ex-lax in the chocolate pudding last summer at the Wari-Bateshwar ruins in Bangladesh?" Suzi retorted. "And there was only *one* bathroom tent for the entire team to share!"

"Uhh . . . I have no idea what you are talking about," Naeem proclaimed sheepishly.

"Ha! Right!" Ty laughed. "Classic, totally classic! I wish we had been there!"

"You did that?" Emma looked at Naeem.

"I *might* have," Naeem replied, trying not to admit to anything.

Suzi wanted to get back to the subject of the cave. "Okay, so, Ty and I were just saying that we need to go back into that cave. I think now, more than ever, we need to find out why this guy is here. It's too much of a coincidence. Why is he snooping around our camp, and why is that cave important to him? I really think it has something to do with the fact that Nefertiti could *possibly* be in there."

"Was it her he was looking for, or was it something else in there he wanted?" Emma asked.

"I don't know, but I really wanna find out," Suzi replied.

"As long as that *something else* is not us," Naeem remarked fearfully.

"Okay, what time are we going to meet tomorrow?" Tyler asked.

"Well, as early as possible, I think," Suzi exclaimed.

But Emma warned, "Look, you guys. They know we snuck out today."

"Who knows?" Naeem's eyes opened wide as he looked around the group. If his father knew, he would be in so much trouble. Last summer's ex-lax escapade put him on serious probation.

"Well, Aunt Mandi did meet us coming back into camp." Tyler reminded them of the close call they'd had earlier.

"And Nora came by our tent a little while ago and told me not to venture out again, with my dad sitting right there! He was not happy with me either," Emma said.

"Okay, guys, look. We need to find out what is so important about that cave," Suzi pushed.

"I am not very happy about making my father mad at me again, but I do want to know what is so important in there," Naeem reluctantly agreed with Suzi.

"Okay, so, are we all in?" asked Suzi.

"Yes, okay. I am in," Naeem said, followed by Tyler, who exclaimed, "I'm in!"

"Me too, but what time?" Emma asked.

"Same time as today?" Tyler suggested.

They all nodded. "Cool!" Tyler replied, and he put his fist in the middle of the group. One by one, they put their hand on his fist and proclaimed their intent to venture out into the cave again.

The four said good night and agreed to keep quiet about what they had seen earlier, their suspicions, and the hat. Naeem and Emma walked away from the Carruth tent, but Emma felt as though they were being watched. She turned to look behind her and noticed they were, in fact, being closely watched . . . by Mandi.

12

Tyler woke very early the next morning to a tugging at his blankets. After a few swats at the tug, he finally heard, "Dude, get up!"

When he sleepily opened one eye, he saw Jake standing over him. Tyler jumped up in his bed. "What? What's going on?"

Jake chuckled and said, "Nothin' man. Get up. You're with me today. We've got a lot to do. Meet me in the research tent in half an hour."

Once his sleepy fog passed and he realized he would be mapping with Jake today instead of running for tools for Nora's crew, Tyler was up, showered, dressed, and had breakfast in less than thirty minutes. He was so excited. As much as his sister loved to dig and brush dirty objects, he loved mapping. Tyler saw mapping as the final link to sorting it all out. He considered himself somewhat of a mapping apprentice. Tyler felt that becoming an Archaeological Mapper would be an acceptable second choice if he didn't make it as a professional hockey player. He worked with his cousin, Jake, several times in the past, and in Tyler's mind, each time was cooler than the one before. Tyler looked up to and admired Jake. And, well, Jake not only saw Tyler as the little brother he never had but also as someone with quite a knack for mapping. Jake didn't mind Tyler being around and actually encouraged it. Tyler had an eye for details, and Jake liked that.

Excited about his outing with Jake, Tyler burst into the research tent as if he'd just run a major race to get there. He tripped over three canisters of maps, then knocked over a small table with a tray of croissants and tea, only to turn and stumble over a box of documents sitting on the floor. As he tried to grab the teapot to prevent it from crashing into a million pieces, he fell backward into yet another box on the floor. He sat inside the box with his legs sticking up in the air, held up the teapot proudly, and then proclaimed, "Got it!"

Jake, Mandi, Asim, and even his mom, Ellie, all stood in complete amazement at the mess Ty had managed to make in a matter of mere seconds. The only one not amazed was Suzi, who walked into the tent just behind Tyler, looked at the mess, and said, "Oh, I see Ty made it on time." Then she stepped over her brother as if he wasn't even there.

Jake and Mandi leaned over to help Tyler out of the box. Suzi grabbed the teapot while Ellie picked up the box that Tyler's butt had just crashed through. Ellie asked, "Suz, go through here and look for the files on Nefertiti for me, please."

Suzi put the teapot on the readjusted table and took the box from her mother. "Sure. No probs!"

By 9:00 a.m., project work was in full force. Based on information and data, Ellie located an area just a couple hundred yards from camp that held promise as a possible burial chamber. The spot was a small entrance just on the north side of the hill where the kids had been the day before. Whether it was Nefertiti's chamber or not was the bigger question. Mandi expressed her doubts as to the authenticity of the location, but Ellie stood firm. However, Mandi's insistence became a source of frustration for Ellie.

How on earth could I be that wrong? All of the evidence points to this specific location . . . This has to be it . . . Where else could it be? Ellie thought to herself. Although Ellie was a force to be reckoned with in the archaeological world, she also knew Mandi was brilliant, which made her second-guess her own findings.

After several hours of back-and-forth assessments, the team finally decided to break for lunch around noon. One by one, the kids began to head into the mess tent. Tyler made no pretense. "I'm starved!"

Suzi followed right behind him. "I could eat two double Dino-Burgers," she remarked.

"A Dino... what?" Emma questioned as she filed in line right behind Suzi.

"Dino-Burger!" Tyler explained. "It's this amazing hamburger place back home."

"It is sooo good!" At this point, the thought of a nice, juicy burger made Suzi's mouth water.

"Okay, well, you guys will have to settle for meatball soup," Nora replied, handing each of them a bowl. Today was Nora's turn to cook. Sometimes, this was good, and well, sometimes not. Everyone took turns, and most of the crew looked forward to Ellie's turn. Even the Egyptian workers loved Ellie's southern cooking. Nora was an outstanding crew chief, but her cooking skills were hit or miss at best, so most everyone was cautious when Nora was in the mess tent.

The look of longing the kids had on their faces only moments ago was gone, and a dose of reality had set in as they looked at the bowls of soup on their trays.

"What's that floating in there?" Suzi questioned and frowned at Nora but was met with a stern look in return. "Oh, my bad. I see now . . . a meatball. Of course, silly me." Suzi lowered her head and quickly walked away.

Just after Suzi, Tyler, and Emma sat down to eat, Naeem came racing to the table. "Hey guys! Hey guys!" He sat down beside them and said, "I was working with my father when he asked Nora if that drifter had come back into camp last night."

"Drifter?" Suzi questioned.

"Yes! Apparently, a man had been seen hanging around the edge of camp. The digging team kicked him out."

Emma asked, "Do you think it was that man from the cave?"

"I'd bet my lunch on it!" Suzi replied.

"Who wants to win that bet?" Tyler retorted.

"Wait. Who has that hat we found?" Emma suddenly realized, "I think we left it lying around somewhere."

"We? Uh, no. You left that stinky thing in our tent last night," Tyler retorted. "And I have it. I stuck it under my bed so no one would find it."

"Whew! Okay." Emma was relieved.

"Alright, let's finish eating and meet back here at 2 o'clock." Naeem went to get his lunch and sat back down with the others. No one said much during lunch, just the soup slurping and short idle conversations. Once they finished lunch, each of them returned to their prospective jobs for the day. Ty went back to following Jake around like a puppy on a leash. Suzi met her mom and Mandi at the dig site, where the debate over Nefertiti's burial location continued. Naeem was fortunate to be helping his dad in the research tent and out of the desert sun. Ahmal had been helping Asim with archiving, and cataloging for the museum. Naeem liked working with Asim, and it was his ambition to be able to work in the Museum's Archives Room when he was older. Emma was in and out of the tent. She went back and forth between Dr. Carruth and her father, bringing delicate pieces to be sorted and cataloged. Emma was not as keen on archaeology as the others. Although she loved hanging out with her dad, she had her heart set on becoming a literature professor at Cambridge. Her mother had been a literature professor there, and, well, she wanted to be one too. Like her mother, she loved to read. Books took her imagination on unbelievable journeys. She was barely fourteen years old but well-read, far past her age. She loved the feminism of Elizabeth Browning and the exotic settings of Rudyard Kipling. She loved it all. Point of fact, her father made her remove several books from her bags before they left. He said they were just "too much." But Emma didn't mind, as long as she had at least two books to keep her company. Yet, so far, she'd been kept too busy to find the time to read.

At 1:45 p.m., the kids began to look around for each other. They were still technically "working," but these obvious glances between each other caught Mandi's attention. *What are they up to?* Mandi thought to herself. Cautiously, she moved from section to section, eyeing the children. The last thing she needed was four teenagers complicating things. She loved these kids dearly but would not let them get in her way.

As fate would have it, Ellie called a meeting, "Mandi, Asim, Jake, and Ahmal, would you all come to the research tent for a brief meeting?"

Mandi hesitated to respond as she continued to attempt to keep a watchful eye on the kids.

"Mandi! Waiting on you . . . " Ellie called out but noticed Mandi staring out into the camp. "What on earth is she staring at?" Ellie whispered to herself.

Mandi broke her concentration and headed for the research tent. As she reached the door, Ellie asked, "Is something wrong out there? What were you staring at so intently?"

"What? Oh, uh, nothing. I was just, uh, making sure the diggers were packing up correctly; that's all," Mandi responded casually as she squeezed by Ellie and entered the tent. Ellie gave a curious look back into camp, shook her head, and went inside for the meeting.

Not long into the meeting, Jake and Mandi began arguing about where evidence showed the main digging should take place. "Look. My calculations, which are based on the evidence, put that chamber right here!" Jake demanded as he pointed to a specific spot on the map.

"I agree with Jake, Mandi. He's *never* been that far off," Ellie defended. "I have looked over the data and the evidence several times. The hieroglyphs suggest it is within only meters of where we are now."

"Look. My sources in Cairo say this is way off. We need to be looking to the east," Mandi demanded.

Meanwhile, outside camp, Nora and her crew were still packing up for the day and were far too busy to notice four young teenagers strolling towards the back of camp. As the kids walked past the research tent, they could hear arguing. This unsettled Suzi. She had never heard a crossword between any of them. They had always been on the same page with everything! Perplexed, Suzi continued to lead the other three out of camp.

13

The afternoon sun was intense, but as the four kids walked into the cave, it was like a giant air conditioner. The temperature must have dropped twenty degrees. "Ahhhhh," Ty sighed. "Feels good in here!"

"Why is it so much cooler in here than outside?" Emma questioned.

"Because there is no sun," Tyler returned.

"Duh," Suzi sarcastically replied.

Slightly irritated at his sister's sarcasm, Tyler responded, "No, I mean the sun heats the earth on the outside. But inside, under the rocks, there are different variables."

The three of them simply stared at Tyler.

"Okay, look," Tyler explained. "Inside a cave, heat comes from different places, depending on the type of rock around the cave. Heat can even come from a river that could run underground, a geothermal gradient, or even any kind of tectonic activity."

The other three continued to look at Tyler like a deer in the headlights. "Uhh, tell me again why your grades are D's and C's?" Suzi remarked. She was every bit as stunned as she was impressed.

Emma and Naeem walked past Tyler and looked at him as if he had turned into some sort of alien. "What?" Tyler responded. "You asked!"

Suzi walked past him and patted him on the back. "Good

job!"

Suzi motioned the others to follow her. Soon, they reached the same crossway of caverns. "Okay, so, Emma, did we go to the right or left yesterday?"

"We went to the left," Emma responded.

"You sure?" Suzi glanced back at her friend.

"Positive. Remember, turning right goes to the edge of the cave. Besides, these pictures are pointing left," Emma reminded them.

"Oh, yeah, right." Suzi motioned to the others to follow her to the left. But just as they turned to the left, all four stopped dead in their tracks. In the middle of the corridor sat a large bag of digging tools that someone had left behind.

"Okay, that was definitely *not* here yesterday," Emma acknowledged.

"Nope," Suzi responded as they all stood frozen.

"What's it doing here?" Ty asked.

"I don't know," Suzi responded again as they all stood perfectly still and continued to stare at the bag of tools.

"Whoever owned these tools might be returning," Naeem's voice trembled.

"Look, we agreed to get to the bottom of this, so let's go on," encouraged Emma.

"Yeah, okay. Let's keep moving," Suzi agreed.

The boys looked at the girls as if they had lost their minds. "Oh, come on. We'll be careful. Sheesh!" Emma said in a loud whisper.

Begrudgingly, the guys shook their heads and agreed. The kids stepped around the tools, careful not to disturb them. "Careful, though. Whoever those belong to doesn't need to know we're here," Suzi advised.

The children continued walking through the cave for quite

some time. Oddly, there was no strange, weird man from yesterday, no voices, and no smell of Grampa's spicy cologne. Nothing. Just the musty smell of an ancient cavern penetrated their noses. Their flashlights were the only light. Without them, the cave would have been as dark as the nothingness of an abyss. With every step, however, the kids became a bit more confident. After all, they had been in there a while, and other than a strange bag of tools lying around, there had been no sign of their friend from yesterday.

"By the way, exactly what is it we are looking *for*?" Emma asked.

"Yeah, Suz. We've been in here for two hours, and all I see is blackness," Tyler said.

"I don't know," Suzi proclaimed.

The other three stopped just ahead of Suzi, turned, and, with a unanimous motion, lit up Suzi's face with flashlights.

"Excuse me?" Tyler quickly responded.

"I'll know it when I see it," Suzi returned.

"You'll know when you see it?" Tyler retorted. "What does that even mean?'

Looking like they had just questioned the unquestionable, Suzi replied. "Oh, come on, guys. Seriously, anything out of the ordinary, hieroglyphics, I guess . . . "

The others had no response, just the blank stare.

Suzi sighed. "Look, we came in here because it was close to where we were digging, hoping to find something that pertains to Nefertiti. But instead, we came across something unexpected," she said.

Naeem interrupted. "Yeah, some man who does not belong here."

Suzi continued reassuringly, "Exactly! Odd, right? I mean, who is he, and why is he here at the same time we are? Okay, that, and wouldn't it be cool if *we* were the ones to find Queen Nefertiti?"

Emma sighed. "Americans are crazy."

Naeem put his hand on her shoulder. "Yes. Yes, they are."

"This cave was your idea in the first place," Suzi replied as she glared at Naeem.

"She's right," Tyler agreed.

"Okay, let's just keep moving," Emma continued. "What do we need to be looking for again? Hieroglyphics?"

"Yeah, but we haven't seen anything," said Tyler.

Suzi stopped to aim her flashlight all around them. She looked up, side to side, forward, and backward. There was nothing. "No, but this cave was clearly used for something. It's too constructed. The walls have clear lines and directions. I can't understand why we haven't seen anything. Nothing, no markings of any kind."

Naeem placed his flashlight in a small hole in the wall about shoulder level. Then, he bent down to tie his shoe. Suddenly, Tyler looked at the hole and questioned, "What's that?"

"What is what?" Naeem questioned.

Just then, it caught Suzi's eye as well. "Right there . . . that hole. The one your flashlight is sitting in. These walls are solid and plain, and suddenly, there is a perfectly round hole the size of a small melon in the middle of all this nothingness," she explained.

Emma walked over, removed the flashlight, and looked inside. "Suzi, come take a look at this."

"Ty, hand me your flashlight; my battery is dying," Suzi asked.

Tyler handed her his flashlight, and she peered through the hole. She quickly noticed every wall was covered in hieroglyphics.

"Wow! This is amazing!" Suzi exclaimed.

Each one took turns looking into the chamber. The hole was only about eight or nine inches wide, but they could see well enough through the opening to know it was a hidden chamber. However, it was too dark to tell exactly what was in there.

"I wonder if this is where she's buried?" Suzi was so excited she could barely breathe. She sat back against the wall, trying to catch her breath.

"I don't know, but we need to get going. It's getting really late," Naeem reminded them of the time.

"Now? You want to leave now?" Suzi exclaimed.

Naeem continued, "We can look again later. Suzi, they will come looking for us if we do not return soon. And being grounded to the camp tomorrow will not help us find out what is inside this room."

"Alright, fine. But until we know what exactly is in there, we need to keep this between us." Suzi was adamant the adults must not know where they'd been. She knew Naeem was right. They'd all be grounded to the camp if their parents found out.

As the four of them turned to make their trek back through the cave the way they came in, Tyler noticed a slightly lit area opposite from where they were heading. "Hey guys, look." He grabbed Naeem's shirt, and the others also stopped to see. "Should we go have a look?" Tyler asked.

"Are you insane?" Emma retorted. "It could be that man!"

"I don't think so." Suzi walked past them to look ahead. "It's sunlight, not a flashlight or lantern. Let's go see where it leads."

Naeem protested, "I'm, getting late . . . parents . . . grounding . . . remember?"

"It'll be fine! Come on!" Tyler pulled his nervous friend along.

As they reached the end of the corridor, they realized that not only did it reach the outside, but base camp was only a hundred yards away. "Hey, there's Mom and Mandi at the dig site," Tyler noticed.

"Shhh! They'll hear us." Suzi continued, "And stay down. They can't know we were here."

One by one, they quickly and quietly shimmied down the small cliff and scurried back to camp. When Suzi was walking back to the tents, she noticed just how close the area her mother and the others were discussing was to the cave they had just been exploring. *Oh wow! This could seriously be it! Suzi thought to herself.*

14

Although desert temperatures reached nearly 100 degrees during the day, evenings were often pleasant and even cool at times. As the night fell, the indigo desert skies were filled with stars scattered like millions of fireflies. Subtle signs of life lit up small areas around camp. Several members of the digging crew built a large fire near the middle of camp. Many gathered around the fire, joking and telling stories of their day. The laughter was loud, and the bond between them was strong. Many of these people had worked together for years, and a core group of them worked with Dr. Carruth or her late husband numerous times. Nora became their crew chief only a few years ago but immediately gained their trust and respect. These men knew Egypt well; these men loved Egypt, and these men *were* Egypt. They'd seen many things in this country, both good and bad. Moments of triumph, as well as times of social unrest. Egypt is a part of who they are. Most were men of strong Muslim faith, devoted to their daily prayers and wonderful illustrations of what it meant to be a *true* Muslim. Some were university-educated, and some were mere laymen workers with families to support. No matter their backgrounds, these were good, hard-working men, and Ellie trusted them completely. This was evident when she sat among them, completely immersed in their laughter and stories. She was not someone they saw as an outsider. She was not part of their culture, yet she was one of them. Ellie never saw herself as the "boss" but instead someone who had a responsibility towards those who worked with her. If one of the workers needed assistance, she'd drop what she was doing to lend a hand. Even if it required a shovel or a better look at an old problem, she never delegated what she could do herself right then. The men respected this and, as a result, were dedicated to her cause and trusted her intentions.

This evening, the men were up a little later than normal. Their laughter seemed contagious as several more group members stepped out to enjoy the evening. Jake and Dr. Nasar walked up and sat on a braided rug next to Nora. Jake raised his mug with a toast, "To Nora . . . may your team have a great day again tomorrow." He pulled his cup to his mouth and mumbled but was clearly understood by all, " . . . and keep you too busy to cook dinner tomorrow." The roar of laughter did not protect Jake from Nora's icy stare, which he tried desperately to ignore.

"Nora, you are indeed a woman of many talents. But your cooking does lack some skill," Ahmal chimed in from the other side of the fire circle and continued. "You all will be happy to know I will cook breakfast and dinner tomorrow. Jake has lunch duty."

The crew clapped with enthusiasm. "Fine, you're all fired," Nora joked. "And what is this culinary masterpiece we will experience tomorrow?"

"Kushari and Aish," Ahmal replied.

The men reacted with a round of applause and excitement. Kushari was a fairly traditional dish in Egypt. It was relatively inexpensive but very popular. Kushari was a mixture of pasta, rice, chickpeas, garlic, black lentils, and a spicy tomato or chili sauce. Aish, however, was a type of pocket bread, a staple in Egyptian culture, and was even sometimes used instead of eating utensils. A wide grin spread across Asim Nasar's face. This was good news. Kushari was one of his favorite dishes. *Emma will be happy too*, he thought to himself.

Mandi was restless and decided to go for a stroll around camp. She paused and leaned against a large boulder next to camp. She could see everyone laughing and enjoying themselves around the campfire. So many things were going through her mind. These were her friends. She had to trust them. But her responsibilities elsewhere required constant caution. She had known Ellie for almost twenty years. Not only were they long-time colleagues, but they were also college roommates and best friends. She was Suzi's godmother and was Ellie's maid of honor at her wedding. But her sense of duty stopped her from trusting the very people she trusted most. She was a part of something no one else understood, and she could not explain. She knew Jake was spot on in his geographical calculations. He always was, but somehow, she had to steer them away. She agreed to take this job to ensure this grave was never located or disturbed. There was just too much at stake. If they found Nefertiti, they would find a secret far bigger than they had bargained for.

Just as Mandi was about to turn in for the night, she saw Suzi sitting alone, reading beside the research tent. Ordinarily, this would amuse her. Mandi usually encouraged Suzi's inquisitions, but now she found herself worried whenever she saw Suzi read, write things down, or talk with the other children secretly. She knew Suzi well. She was just like her mother—brilliant, only ten times more relentless, which worried Mandi immensely. Mandi decided to walk over and see what Suzi was up to.

"Hey, Doodle."

"Hey," Suzi responded.

"Whatcha readin'?" Mandi asked as she sat down next to her Goddaughter.

"Nothing really, just some old notes on Nefertiti," Suzi responded.

"Ahh, anything interesting?" Mandi asked, then noticed a few maps sitting beside her as well. "What are these?"

"It's just some old stuff my dad had," Suzi replied. "Nothing major."

"Where are your partners in crime?" Mandi asked and looked around the camp.

"Ty fell asleep right after dinner. A shame, really; he would've loved this campfire. I thought about waking him up," Suzi explained.

"Why didn't you?" Mandi asked.

"Cause . . . he was tired. He worked really hard today. The other two are around here somewhere. I think Emma is reading in her tent, and Naeem is reorganizing some tools for tomorrow. He'll probably be out here soon."

"I see" Mandi responded but wanted to ask more. "So, where did you guys go off to today?"

Suzi looked at Mandi. Mandi was someone she had a hard time reading. Her mom, Ty, Naeem, Ahmal, and even Emma were all easy enough to read. And she could always read her dad. But Mandi . . . Mandi was different. Suzi could never quite figure Aunt Mandi out. She was like a haze Suzi could never quite see through. "I don't think I know what you mean?"

"You guys left camp just after lunch again today," Mandi replied.

"Oh, umm . . . we just went looking around. No big deal." Suzi tried to play it off but knew they had been told not to venture off.

Mandi's disapproving scowl was only offset by her response. "You guys were told not to go out and about. I know you heard about the uninvited visitor we had late yesterday afternoon." Mandi then shifted her position to look straight at her goddaughter. "Okay, I'm not going to tell your mother, but don't let me catch you guys heading out again."

Mandi hoped her words would have the intended impact. But she knew her goddaughter was far too inquisitive to just walk away from her curiosity. Suzi reluctantly agreed, hugged her godmother good night, and walked towards her tent. Just as she approached her tent, Suzi looked back at Mandi. She was unnerved when she realized Mandi was still watching her. Suzi stepped inside the tent but hid just in the shadows of the doorway. She gazed back into the night and watched as Mandi finally walked away. Mandi didn't walk towards her tent, however. She headed in the complete opposite direction.

In the meantime, Tyler woke up to see his sister hiding behind the flap of their tent. He quietly got up and walked over to see what she was looking at. He stood right behind her and looked outside.

"Who are you spying on?" Ty whispered.

Not realizing he was even awake, Suzi jumped. "Hooooly crap!" She gave a backhanded swat at her brother. "Are you crazy? Geez! You nearly scared the mess out of me! Don't sneak up on people like that!"

But, by the time she had looked back out of the tent, Mandi had disappeared. "Wait, where'd she go?"

"Where did *who* go?" Ty whispered again, as he stuck his head in front of his sisters to see out the tent.

Suzi grabbed the back of her brother's shirt and pulled him back in. "No one."

"No one? Really?" Ty glared. He knew she was lying.

Nervously, Suzi sorted through her suitcase to look for her

sleeping sweats. Ty walked past her and rolled his eyes, "Uh huh, no one. Yeah right."

"Nope, no one," Suzi simply stated and continued to fumble with her sweats.

Ty laid back down on his cot and pretended to go back to sleep. He watched out the corner of his partially closed eyelid as his sister snuck out of the tent. He jumped up, hurried to the door flap, and watched as she headed off towards the back side of camp. He knew his sister was someone who could definitely take care of herself in most situations, but this made him part curious and part nervous. He slipped on his sneakers and followed her. After all, what are brothers for, right?

Ty watched her weave between tents and finally caught up with her peeking around the mess tent obviously watching someone. He came up behind her, trying to see who she was watching. "Is that Aunt Mandi?" Ty whispered.

Again, Suzi jumped. "Seriously? What are you? Some kind of freakin' ninja?" Suzi hissed. "And why are you here? You should be in bed." Suzi turned back to look at Mandi.

"So should you! And no one? Who are you kidding? You're 'bout as slick as a goat," Ty replied, louder than Suzi appreciated.

"Shhhh!" Suzi whipped around with a finger on her lips and a stern frown at her brother.

"Who's she talking to?" Ty whispered quietly.

"I have no idea, but I haven't seen him around here before. He seems as nervous as she does."

"She does seem kinda squirrely," Ty noticed.

"Yep, and that's not like her."

"No, it's not," Ty agreed.

The older man appeared to be in his late 60s. Dapper and refined, he was clearly not someone who was part of the excavation team. His European well-tailored suit stood out against the dusty desert. Even though it was hard to see in the dark, he seemed vaguely familiar to Suzi.

Suddenly, the well-dressed man put his jacket and hat on, turned to Mandi, and said, "Find her before they do, please!" He then turned and climbed into the passenger side of the jeep they had been standing next to. The driver sped back up the road. Mandi stood there for several minutes before she headed back into camp. The kids watched as she walked back through the maze of tents. She said good night to Jake and Asim, who were still sitting around the fire, and then walked a few feet to her tent. Suzi and Ty watched as the light dimmed and her tent went dark.

15

Two days later

The sun seemed unusually bright this morning, and the desert heated up quickly. The usual bustle of workers getting tools together broke the silence of the morning. Nora began assigning duties to the various digging teams.

Jake and Ahmal had previously pulled several maps and laid each one out neatly on an individual table. Naeem and Ty walked up carrying a box of Jake's surveying tools and scopes.

"Hey guys, put those next to my backpack. I need to pull a few of those this morning. Mandi swears I'm off in my calculations. I need to see what she's thinking." Jake continued, "Ty, you with me today?"

"Heck yeah! And, if Ahmal doesn't need Naeem today, can he come too?" Tyler responded.

Jake glanced over to Ahmal. Ahmal gave a reluctant but approving nod.

"Sure, an extra set of hands would be great. If you're not busy today, Ahmal, I could really use your familiar eye on this stuff too," Jake asked and packed the last of his tools into his bag.

Excited, the boys ran off to grab their backpacks. Ahmal glanced back towards Mandi, then replied, "Yes, I think that is a good idea." He walked close to Jake so that a whisper was all that was needed. "Look. I have known Mandisa for many years and have never known her to be wrong. But this time, I think you are correct."

Jake slapped Ahmal on the back and said, "Then, let's go find out for sure." The two walked away from the research station. Suddenly, Jake remembered the notebook Ellie had given him the night before to recalculate his data and location. "Hey, Ahmal, grab that black notebook, would ya'?" Ahmal grabbed the notebook quickly but didn't realize a few pieces of paper accidentally slipped out onto the ground as they walked away toward the jeep.

As the boys approached the research station, they saw the papers fall out onto the ground. They tried to get Ahmal's attention but were not successful. Naeem gathered the papers. "We need to get this to Papa and Jake."

"Wait, was that Mom's Data Notebook in his hands?" Ty asked, stopping his friend from taking another step.

"Yes, so . . . ?" Naeem looked back.

Without explanation, Ty grabbed the papers from Naeem and began to look them over. His expression changed as his eyes widened.

"Do you know what you are looking at?" Naeem asked.

"No, not really. But I recognized some markings on this paper from that little room we saw through that hole yesterday. I think they may be related." Quickly, he pulled out a notepad from his backpack and jotted down as much information as possible from the papers.

Naeem looked at his friend with both amazement and horror. "You are getting more like your sister every day."

Ty looked up at him, "Definitely not funny. Come on, let's catch up to your dad and Jake."

The boys soon caught up to Jake and Ahmal. "These fell out of that notebook!" Ty handed Jake the dropped papers from the notebook.

"Oh, hey, thanks, man," Jake said as he stuffed them back into Ellie's notebook.

"Oh, dang! I forgot my water bottle. I'll be right back," Ty exclaimed. "Oh, me too!" Naeem yelled as he followed Ty back down the path.

"Wait, what? Oh, come on, guys. Hurry up!" Slightly frustrated, Jake and Ahmal loaded the rest of the tools into the Jeep.

Meanwhile, back at the dig site, Suzi and her mom were busy brushing off some pottery the diggers found the day before and cataloging them separately on the research table. Suddenly, Ty and Naeem ran recklessly into the workstation.

"Careful!" Ellie exclaimed, just as the boys almost slid into a table of priceless pieces of Egyptian pottery.

Suzi gasped, closed her eyes, and waited for the crash. Then, she opened one eye as the guys stopped just shy of the artifacts. The sound of relief resonated as Ellie began to breathe once again.

"What on earth?" Ellie scolded. "You two know better than to run in this area!"

Suzi stared at Naeem and Ty wide-eyed, "What do you guys want?"

"Oh, uh, Mom. I need to take Suzi to the other side of camp. Uh . . . um," Ty stammered, "I saw something cool there!" Ty got a big smile on his face, proud of his response at the moment.

"Oh, really. What is it? And I thought you two went with Jake?" Ellie asked.

"It's a desert monitor," Naeem chimed in. "And well, we just haven't left yet."

"A monitor?!" Ellie exclaimed. "You two need to stay away from that thing! Let the crew shoo it away."

"Oh, yeah, they're about to, but we thought Suzi might want to see it before they did. Uh, from a distance, of course," Naeem continued with a grin that even the Cheshire Cat would have found impressive.

Suzi suddenly noticed Ty's look of urgency and played along. "Oh wow! Cool! Hey, Mom, I'll be right back. It'll only take a second." Without waiting for permission, Suzi ran off with Naeem and Ty right beside her.

"But . . . uh . . . wait . . . oh, fine . . . hurry back please!" Ellie protested and then returned to brushing and arranging the artifacts into sections.

As the three rounded the mess tent, the smell of fresh bread baking over a fire permeated the air like Fadil's Bakery in town. Ty was immediately distracted.

"Snap out of it!" Suzi snapped her fingers before her brother's nose to reel him back in from the bakery abyss.

"Oh, right, sorry. Here, take these. They were in that data notebook Mom guards with her life," Ty said proudly. He handed his find over to his sister as if she were the leader of the CIA, and he had just secured top-secret Russian documents.

"How did you get these?" Suzi asked wide-eyed as she noticed the hieroglyphic writings.

"Mom let Jake use her notebook to recheck his calculations, and some papers accidentally slipped out. I wrote everything down on this notepad so I could return the papers to Jake without anyone noticing they were missing." Ty continued proudly, "It's the same writings we saw in that hole yesterday."

"Cool," Suzi said. Her eyes glued to the notepad, she slowly walked back to her mother and their work.

"Cool? That's all she's got? I bring her information from a book she hasn't been able to come within thirty feet of, and all she can say is . . . *Cool*?" Ty exclaimed in disbelief.

"Come on, man. Dad and Jake are waiting," said Naeem.

"Yeah, okay. But cool? Really?" Ty continued to complain as he followed behind Naeem.

Ty and Naeem headed back to the other side of camp to meet Jake and Ahmal, who had begun to get impatient. "Come on, you two! Hurry up!" Jake yelled across the camp.

The boys panted as they ran to the Jeep where Jake and Ahmal waited.

"Where's your water?" Jake asked.

"Oh, uhhh, in our backpacks. It was there all along. We just didn't realize we put it in there already," Ty replied.

"Uh-huh . . . " Ahmal responded suspiciously.

Ty and Naeem took one more glance of relief at one another and climbed into the back of the Jeep.

The four of them drove to the far outskirts of the dig site. The hill on the back edge of the camp was the best vantage point for Jake to set up his equipment.

As they reached the plateau, Jake stopped the Jeep, set the parking brake, and looked at Ahmal. "Well, let's see where I made a mistake."

Ahmal responded quickly, "You do not make mistakes, my friend."

Jake stepped out of the Jeep. "I guess there's a first time for everything."

Ty jumped out of the back of the Jeep, grabbed the folded tripod, and said, "Ahmal's right, Jake. Your mistakes are misspelled words or un-erased smudges on your maps. Not geospatial calculations."

Naeem looked at his dad. "Did he just say, 'geospatial calculations'?"

Completely speechless, all three of them stared at Tyler.

Utterly amused, Jake replied, "Thank you for that, Ty. But

something is either off with *my* work or Mandi's. We need to get this sorted out soon."

Naeem grabbed the wide-angle lens case and water rations from the Jeep. He walked past Ty, who was unfolding the tripod. "Nerd."

Ty looked up. "What . . . ?"

Slinging his backpack over his shoulder, Jake stopped to look at Ty, "Next time Aunt Ellie tells me you're getting Ds in school, I'm coming down to Charlotte to kick your butt personally. Got it?"

Soberly, Ty looked up to Jake and replied, "Yeah, got it."

Jake put his arm around Ty's neck, ruffled his cousin's hair, and then ran to catch up with Ahmal and Naeem. The four of them walked to the edge of the hill to set up Jake's surveying equipment. Jake wanted to make sure everything was set and ready by noon. He felt the shadows would be minimal at that time of day, and nothing would be left to chance. The guys took notes, calculated data, and rechecked the map's locations for over an hour.

"I don't get it. Everything is exactly as it should be," Jake said.

Ahmal looked at his friend. "See, I told you. It is Mandisa's error. Not yours."

"So it seems. Hey, man, when you tell Mandi, be easy. She doesn't take bad news too well," Jake said.

"Hahaha, uh nope. I am not paid hazard pay. That is all you, my friend!" Ahmal continued to laugh and waved to the boys. "Naeem! You and Ty start putting this equipment back into the Jeep."

Bewildered, Jake sighed. "Thanks, *friend*. I appreciate the support." Ahmal continued to laugh and waved as he walked back to the Jeep.

Once the equipment was loaded back into the Jeep, Jake pulled Ahmal off to the side out of earshot of the boys. "Hey man, so I keep getting a weird feeling about Mandi. It's like she's not on the same page as everyone else," Jake confided to Ahmal.

"I agree. Have you talked to your aunt about it?" Ahmal asked.

"No," Jake replied.

"Perhaps you should. Maybe she knows something you do not," Ahmal continued. "Mandisa takes her work very seriously and is not usually so far off. And oddly, she is never this stubborn! I told you before that your calculations and surveys have been right on target. Something tells me Mandi knows it as well."

Jake looked at his friend and sighed with a nod of agreement.

<h1 style="text-align:center">16</h1>

The day progressed, and the kids found no time to take their next trip into the cave. They made especially sure to avoid the tent where the adults debated the location issue most of the day after Ahmal and Jake returned from their hilltop survey. The debate became rather loud at times. And although her curiosity started to get the best of her, even Suzi knew it was best to just steer clear for a while.

"Mandi, I'm sorry. But I'm telling you my calculations are correct. Your sources are wrong. Based on the data collected from these sources." Jake dropped a stack of files on the table. "And the hieroglyphs hidden in a small priest's room at Amarna's Great Aten Temple, this is it. It should be less than one kilometer from here, just east of this camp." Jake pointed to the location on the most recent map he created.

"Jake, I have Egyptian resources that you don't. The chatter around my circles tells me it's to the west." Mandi then pointed to a different spot on the map.

"I understand you have more inside info, but—" Jake argued.

"Mandisa." Ahmal interrupted and placed both hands on the map between them. "In all the years we have worked side by side, I have always known you to be correct with your speculations. But I have also never known you to follow an inside source without comparing it to proven scientific information." He continued, "Why are you insistent that your *sources* are correct and the information your colleagues have collected and researched are wrong?"

Mandi became angry and looked around the tent at Ellie, Ahmal, and Jake. "I don't understand why you all don't trust me!" Then she stormed out of the tent.

Ellie looked at the rest of the team. "Jake, you've calculated and recalculated. . . correct?"

"Yes," he replied.

"I was there. He is absolutely on the right track with this," Ahmal replied in support.

She looked over to Asim and Nora, silently sitting off to the side. "You two have stayed relatively quiet. What do you think?" Ellie continued, "Should we proceed with the information at hand or follow Mandi's inside sources? Which, by the way, who are they? Do you know these people? Are they reputable?"

Asim walked over to the table where the map was spread out like a giant tablecloth. He placed his hands on his hips and looked it over. "You know I am new to this team, so I have kept to myself. Whether we proceed or not is not up to me. However, there is something to be said for local lore. It is my understanding that a group of Bedouin shepherds accidentally came across the possible burial site. There was, in fact, a great deal of talk around the blood antiquities community about this sighting. But I do not have any proof, only hearsay."

"Do you think this is the same hearsay Mandi is relying on?" Jake chimed in.

"Perhaps. But I trust Mandi and her sources. However, the decision is yours, Ellie," Asim cautiously responded.

"Yeah, well, I'll think it over. Whatever we do, we need to move forward tomorrow. We wasted too much time on this. I don't want to waste anymore. I'll have a talk with Mandi tonight."

Dr. Carruth walked out of the tent to go look for her old friend. The rest of the team simply looked at one another for a few moments then began to pick up and put away the maps and documents that had been dragged out during the debate.

Shortly after leaving the tent, Ellie saw the kids sitting around a table just outside the mess tent. "Waiting on the dinner bell, are we?" She sat down next to Tyler and asked, "What've you all been doing all day?" She seemed to relax and enjoy the moments away from all the discussions for a while. Ty began to rattle on about how cool it was that Jake asked him to tag along today and how much he needed his help.

Suzi rolled her eyes slightly. "Yeah, to hold the 3D scanner and leveling rods."

Ellie cut her eyes at her daughter. "Did anyone downplay you holding trowels and brushes when you were getting started?"

"Besides, I'll have you know, Jake let me set up the Total Station instrument this morning, all by myself," Ty retorted. "It's a surveying tool . . ."

Suzi interrupted, "Yeah, yeah . . . I know what it is," she sighed.

"See, there you have it. Ty, you'll be a mapper before you know it." Ellie continued, "Okay, you four stay out of trouble. I need to go find Mandi."

"Mom, she looked really upset. Is everything okay?" Suzi was concerned.

"Yeah, it's fine. She just isn't seeing eye to eye with the rest of the team on this one, is all. But we'll get it all sorted out," Ellie continued. "Did you see where she went?"

"That way, towards her tent." Suzi pointed to the sleeping tents.

"Ah, thanks. I'll just go have a chat with her. I'll see you four at dinner."

"Okay," Suzi replied.

As soon as their mom was out of earshot, Ty looked at his sister. "Your godmother is acting super weird."

Emma turned to Suzi. "Wait, who's your godmother?"

"Mandi," Suzi continued. "I agree. It's not like her to be so flakey."

"Mandi is your godmother?" Emma interrupted."Yes," Suzi replied casually then turned to look at Naeem. "Has your dad said anything?"

Before Naeem could answer, Emma chimed in again. "That explains a lot."

"Explains what?" Suzi asked.

"Well, earlier today, I heard her talking to my father about her 'goddaughter.'"

"What'd they say?" Ty asked before Suzi could even take a breath.

"Papa said something about 'your goddaughter,' but honestly, I was napping and only heard small bits and pieces of their conversation. But I also heard him say something about her catching us returning from the cave. And that she needs to find out what we're up to."

At that moment, a cowbell interrupted the conversation.

"Finally! Let's walk and talk. I'm hungry," Ty proclaimed.

The other three all replied at the same time. "You're always hungry!"

"Yeah, so. Your point?" Ty defended.

"Come on, guys, let's go," Suzi snickered. "I'm hungry too." The four of them got up and walked into the mess tent.

Naeem spoke first, "My dad says Mandi is way off, and that is not like her."

"Yeah, we heard him and Jake talking," Ty continued. "Jake checked those coordinates twice today. Everything is correct based on the information the team has."

"Well, Aunt Mandi is really pushing another direction. I wonder why?" Suzi insisted. "We need to figure it out."

"Why do *we* need to figure it out?" Emma asked.

Naeem looked at Emma. "Ha! I have learned to *never* ask that question." He placed his hand on Emma's shoulder. "Just go with it."

As the kids entered the tent, the smell was amazing! "No way dinner smells this good. It's Nora's night to cook again," Ty said, in awe of the aroma that filled the air.

Emma replied, "Nora was in the big meeting with your mom and everyone. I think Dad mentioned Sandi was going to cook tonight."

"Who's Sandi?" Ty asked.

"My dad's assistant."

"Ohhh! Well, your dad's assistant can cook anytime she wants!" Ty insisted.

"Definitely!" Naeem agreed. "But Sandi . . . is a *he*."

"Oh! Cool," Ty replied.

Based on the amazing smell, the kids agreed that Sandi was a wonderful substitute cook and proceeded to move quickly over to the plates and utensils so they could dig into the food that smelled so good!

Meanwhile, Ellie found Mandi sitting on a rock watching the sunset over the desert. Realizing Mandi was in deep thought, Ellie recalled an occasion when she approached Mandi from the back while her mind was elsewhere once in college. Ellie ended up flat on her back on the floor of the Oxford Library. Remembering Mandi's serious martial arts skills, Ellie decided to approach her friend from the side, which was always a good decision.

"Hey, you," Ellie said.

"Hey, you," Mandi replied.

"You okay?" Ellie asked.

"Yeah, I'm fine."

"Wanna talk?"

"Not really."

"We need to though."

"Yeah, I know. But I'm just not ready right now."

"I understand. But you should also know that we're probably going to proceed as planned tomorrow afternoon," Ellie replied carefully.

"I figured," Mandi continued to stare off into the Egyptian sunset.

Ellie reached over and hugged her friend, then turned to walk away.

"Ell . . ." Mandi paused as Ellie stopped and looked back at her old friend. "There are forces out there— in these caves— that you cannot begin to understand. Please be careful," Mandi advised.

Looking a bit perplexed, Ellie simply said, "Forces? What kind of forces?"

"Listen, it's more than I can go into at the moment. But you have to trust me . . . " Mandi was interrupted by a desperate call from Suzi who was yelling from the front of the mess tent.

"Mom! Mom!"

"What is it? I'm busy!" Ellie replied.

"It's Ty! He's choking!"

"WHAT!" Ellie quickly turned back to Mandi. "This conversation isn't finished." Then she ran to find her son.

"I have no doubt," Mandi mumbled to herself. When Ellie

was clearly out of view, Mandi grabbed her cell phone from the leg pocket of her cargo shorts and dialed. "I need your help now. You can no longer stay in the background."

"*I understand,*" The voice on the other end of the phone agreed, and Mandi placed the phone back into her pants pocket and walked to the mess tent to check on Tyler.

Ellie barreled into the mess tent. "Tyler! Son! What on earth happened?" She found him sitting on the bench next to the table. He had been well tended to by Lateef, one of the diggers.

Ellie grabbed Tyler up and held him. "Umm, not breathing!" Ty exclaimed. "Too tight, Mom."

"What? Oh right, sorry," Ellie continued. "You scared me half to death!"

"He will be okay, Dr. Carruth. He just got a piece of bread caught in his throat. I was able to give his stomach a little push and out it came. I believe you call it a Heimlich," Lateef said with a smile and a wink.

"Yes. Yes, it is." Ellie laughed nervously. "Thank you so much, Lateef!" Ellie gave Lateef a huge hug. "I am just so grateful!"

"Dr. Carruth, it was no problem. I am glad we were still here. We were just about to leave. Are you okay now, my young man?"

"Yeah. Thanks, dude!" Ty replied.

"You are most welcome." Lateef bowed his head slightly and met up with his friends as they were leaving the tent.

Ellie was watching Lateef and his coworkers leave when she noticed Mandi in the doorway, looking in. Mandi wanted to make sure Tyler was alright, but then she quickly walked away.

<h1 style="text-align:center">17</h1>

The next day

With the next excavation phase underway, it was time for the team to rebuild its food rations and supplies. It was impossible to carry all the food and supplies the team needed for the entire excavation. It was generally Ahmal's job to go across the river to nearby Luxor to get provisions for the team. Parts of Luxor, much like Cairo, were bustling with lots of people, cars, and tourists. Ahmal did not like the overcrowded large cities, so he generally tried to get into the city, get what he needed, and get out quickly.

As the sun rose across the Sahara, Ahmal gathered his backpack and headed to the Jeep. Naeem followed his dad and asked, "Papa! Can I come with you today?"

"Why do you want to come with me this morning? Don't you four have *plans* today?" Ahmal teased as he threw his backpack into the back seat.

"Uh, plans? I am not sure what you mean, Papa." Naeem tried desperately to deflect any possible involvement in mischief.

"Uh-huh. . . " Ahmal replied. "That is fine. Hop in." Glad to be exiting camp for a few hours, Naeem quickly jumped into the passenger seat and shut the door. "Thanks, Papa!"

"Jake!" Ahmal yelled back over his shoulder to Jake who had been chatting with a few diggers next to the supply tent.

"Yeah?"

"Let Dr. Carruth and Nora know Naeem is going with me to Luxor."

"Okay! Will do!"

Ahmal waved to Jake and the crew, then headed up the road towards Luxor.

El-Souk Luxor Market

The Luxor Market was a bustling montage of vendors, farmers, and artisans. Ahmal tried to visit the market only on Tuesdays. Tuesday was the day of the week when most of the farmers brought their fresh fruits and vegetables to sell. Therefore, it was the day of the week when one would find the freshest groceries and the best selections. The various smells and aromas were almost intoxicating. Street vendors cooked some of Egypt's most enticing foods and sweets. Egyptians love desserts and sweets. And the Luxor Market had an array of various bakers peddling their confections. There were also many cafés and stores that offered delicious coffee and food, and a vast assortment of souvenir vendors and shops lined every street.

Next to the market, the museum often used a facility to purchase many of the basic excavation supplies. Ahmal could acquire items such as meat, rice, wheat flour, nuts, dates, breads, and other basic food staples there.

"Naeem, take this money and go over to Fadil's Café. Get the crew some nice desserts." Ahmal handed Naeem several bills of the Egyptian Pound, the currency of Egypt. "I am going next door to the warehouse to pick up our supplies. You wait inside Fadil's until I come back to get you. Do you understand?"

"Yes, Papa." Naeem took the bills and scurried over to Fadil's Café. He absolutely loved going to Fadil's. It always smelled so good in there!

"Naeem! How are you, my boy?" Fadil Nazari, a kind and unassuming man, generally worked up at the front of the café. He loved greeting his customers himself. Just to the right of the front door, several tables and chairs were arranged so that locals and tourists alike could sit and enjoy the sights, sounds, and smells of the Luxor market from the comfort of the open inside patio at Fadil's café. A large glass counter showcased the many delights Fadil had to offer. On display were breads, sandwiches, and sweets of all varieties.

"Hi Fadil, I'm doing well! Papa sent me in to pick out some desserts for the crew."

"Excellent! What would you like for me to pack up for you today?"

Naeem placed both hands on the display case, and his nose was so close that he nearly fogged the glass. He looked over every dessert, and his mouth watered at the thought of sampling every single one of them. "Ohh, hmm . . . I do not know. What is good today?"

"Well, the baklava is very fresh. Made a large batch just this morning!" Fadil replied with a large, pleasant smile.

"Excellent! Then I will take six dozen baklava. Oh, and six dozen of the fatir as well."

"Very well. I will get you the fresh ones from the kitchen. I shall be right back." Fadil winked at Naeem and walked away.

"Thank you!"

Standing near the display case while waiting for Fadil to return, Naeem continued to admire Fadil's delicious pastries. He could not decide which one would most likely be his favorite. *That one! Nooo, definitely this one!* Naeem thought to himself as he scanned from one delicacy to the next. Suddenly, through the glass, he noticed the reflection of two men sitting at a table just a few feet from the door. They were arguing intensely. He turned to look but was quickly spooked when he recognized one of the men at the table. It was the same man who followed them in the cave nearly a week ago. Breathless, he jumped to hide behind an indoor plant next to the door. His face was pale, and he could hardly breathe. He stood practically frozen, only a few feet away, and could hear them arguing.

"He isn't happy!" said the younger man, with a strong French accent.

"I can't bloody well help it, André! I can't get into the camp to get the research!" the Englishman complained. "They've got guards posted everywhere. I tried once already and was caught."

"That is because you are an idiot. I should go in and just grab the artifact. I do not need any research."

"You *grabbed* it once already, remember? That didn't turn out so bloomin' well, did it?"

"That was unavoidable. He fought back."

"And what happened after that? Huh? It mysteriously disappeared from your hotel room! Besides, we need the research to see if there is more treasure there."

The Frenchman gave a seething glare and replied, "Look, Cobb. I know who took it, and if I can get into that camp, I WILL have a little chat with her!"

Cobb was not having any of it. "Right then. Well, that's all we need: more bloodshed. Besides, I think I recognized two of those kids in the cave that day I was there having a look around. I think they are Collin Carruth's grandkids. I met 'em once at a museum."

Fadil's voice broke Naeem's concentration. "Are you okay,

my boy?"

"Uh, yes. Yes, I am fine!" Naeem quickly jumped away from the plant and pulled his baseball cap low over his face in an attempt to disguise himself from the two men he had been eavesdropping on.

Fadil looked at Naeem with concern as he handed him two large bags of pastries. Naeem quickly paid Fadil the money his father gave him, took the bags of pastries, and scurried out of the shop. He completely forgot that he had been instructed to wait inside for his father.

Fadil watched as Naeem ran across the street to the market but became extremely concerned when he looked back inside and recognized the men Naeem had been spying on. Fadil picked up his cell phone from behind the counter and dialed.

Moments later, in the street in front of the market, Naeem literally ran right into his father as he fled Fadil's shop and nearly dropped the bag of pastries. "Naeem! What is the matter with you?! Be careful! You could have hurt someone! I told you to wait until I came for you at Fadil's!"

Pale and breathless. "Yes, Papa. I am so sorry," Naeem replied, looking back at the bakery.

Ahmal realized his son looked extremely frightened. He knelt down. "Are you okay?" he asked.

Naeem looked back at the shop again to ensure he was not followed or being watched. "Yes, Papa," he replied anxiously.

Unsure what to believe, Ahmal took the pastry bags from Naeem, put his hand around his son's shoulders, and walked back toward the Jeep. Ahmal glanced over his shoulder for a quick concerned look at Fadil's pastry shop.

Ahmal and Naeem pulled back into base camp by late afternoon, and Asim came to greet them. "Did you find everything you needed?" Asim asked, noticing Naeem seemed a bit pale and shaken.

"Are you alright, my boy?" he asked.

Naeem did not respond; he just grabbed his backpack, the bags of pastries, and then ran into camp. Asim looked at Ahmal. "Rough ride? You didn't encounter any drifters along the way, did you?"

"No, but something spooked him in town. I have no idea what because he won't talk about it, but definitely something." Ahmal grabbed his backpack and then called out in Arabic. "Lateef, Rashidi! Come! Unload the Jeep. Take these boxes to the supply tent!"

The workers waved and made their way to the Jeep. Asim watched closely as his friend, Ahmal, walked back toward camp.

18

While Naeem and Ahmal were gathering supplies from Luxor, the team had been out working for several hours. Against Mandi's wishes, the rest of the team decided to follow Jake's calculations, which placed them at the base of the mountain where the kids found the entrance to the cave. The day was filled with active digging, which kept Suzi and Emma extremely busy. They barely left the dig site and had no time to roam on their own.

With every passing moment, Ellie found herself more and more excited about the artifacts they had located so far. One item was of particular interest to her. It was a stone tablet about eighteen by twenty-four inches in size etched with hieroglyphics. It looked to be the work of 18th-century dynasty priests. This was the first time since the excavation started that they had found any evidence of real significance. Ellie was more certain than ever that they were indeed on the right track.

Although Mandi was as excited as everyone else about the artifacts they'd uncovered, she grew more and more concerned. She needed to get inside the cave before the rest of the team. She had a job to do. People were depending on her, and time was running out.

As they began to wrap things up for the day, chatter filled the camp, and the evening was full of laughter and promise. Everyone enjoyed dinner, especially the fresh pastries Naeem secured from Fadil's Bakery earlier. Suzi, Tyler, and Emma sat at their usual table. They had worked hard all day and, like everyone else, scarfed down dinner.

With a mouth full of food, Tyler asked, "Has anyone seen Naeem? I haven't seen him since he left for the city this morning."

"That's strange, neither have I. Papa said they left right after breakfast," Emma responded. "Be careful. Don't talk with your mouth full; you'll choke again!"

"My bad!" Ty replied.

Suzi chimed in. "Actually, I saw him for a second this afternoon. He was heading in here with a few boxes from the supply tent, so I know they're back."

As if on cue, Naeem opened the flap of the mess tent. "Hey! There he is!" Tyler exclaimed.

Naeem walked over to his friends and plopped down on the bench. He looked tired. They all did. But Naeem looked like he'd really had a rough day.

"Hey, dude, you hungry? I'm going to grab more stew. You want some?" Suzi offered.

"Yes," he simply replied, following Suzi to the chow line.

As they were standing in line for stew, Naeem leaned forward to whisper to Suzi. "I need to tell you something."

Suzi turned and looked at him. "Oh, yeah? What?" she whispered back.

"I will tell you guys after dinner," he said.

"Maaaybe you could tell me now," Suzi responded.

"I cannot. I need to wait."

"Okay, fine. But you don't just tell someone you have to tell them something, then say, '*I'll tell you later*.'"

"Sorry," Naeem sighed. He took the bowl of stew the cook handed him and returned to the table.

Suzi stared at Naeem as he headed back to the table. He

looked stressed. Concerned, she also watched him throughout dinner. Suzi noticed that she wasn't the only one watching Naeem. Mandi and Asim were seated together only a few tables over. Suzi became aware that they were not only watching Naeem; they were also having a deep conversation.

After dinner, Nora and a few workers built another big bonfire in the middle of camp. The kids found themselves a nice big rock near the fire and climbed on top.

"I had a problem in the city today," Naeem finally admitted.

The other three turned their heads to Naeem in surprise. "What kind of *problem*?" Emma asked.

"Yeah, dude, you okay?" Ty asked.

"Yes, but I saw that man we ran into in the cave," Naeem said.

Suzi and Ty looked at one another and then back at Naeem. "Wait, what? Where did you see him?" Suzi asked.

"At Fadil's," Naeem said.

"Aw, man! Love that place!" Tyler exclaimed. The others looked at Ty. "What? Fadil is a genius!" He replied.

"Yes, well, my father sent me there to pick up desserts for the crew. While I was waiting on Fadil to get them from the back," Naeem continued, "I heard two men arguing. I looked over, and there he was!"

"If one was the man from the cave, then who was the other one?" Emma asked.

"I do not know. But the man from the cave said he had been trying to get into the camp to retrieve some kind of artifact and research. The other man was . . . French, I think. He looked really mean and said he wanted to come into camp himself, to retrieve the artifact."

"We have lots of artifacts here." Emma continued, "What could he possibly want?"

"I do not know. But the man we saw in the cave said there had been enough bloodshed and that he also wanted our research to see if there was more treasure here." Naeem looked afraid but continued. "Then Fadil came out with the baklava, so I grabbed the bags and ran out of the shop."

"Bloodshed!" Ty exclaimed.

"Yes! The mean one also said that he knew who took this artifact from him, and it sounded like he wanted revenge on someone here in the camp!"

"I wonder who he's after?" Suzi remarked.

"I do not know, but he referred to this person as *her*," Naeem said.

The kids looked around trying to figure out who it could be. They looked at everyone with suspicion.

"The only one acting a little squirrely here is Aunt Mandi," Tyler whispered.

"That's true. I've never seen her act so weird," Suzi agreed.

As the four of them looked over at Mandi, they noticed her staring back at them. Awkwardly and quickly, they looked away.

"Well, Mandi gets my vote," Ty said.

"Mine too," Naeem chimed in.

Emma just looked at her friend. "Suzi, I agree with them."

Suzi looked at the others, but her heart was breaking. Mandi had been like a favorite aunt to her. She called Mandi with boy troubles, when she won awards, and when she was frustrated with her mother. Mandi was always there with words of wisdom, but now it was as if she hardly knew her.

"Before we jump to any conclusions, let's try to break away and go back into the cave tomorrow, first thing in the morning, before breakfast. Hopefully, we'll find some answers there." Suzi wanted to be certain if she was going to accuse her godmother of anything.

"I do not know Suzi. These men were really scary!" Naeem protested.

"I agree with Suzi. What makes them so interested in *this* dig?" Ty said.

"Um, excuse me. These men referred to BLOODSHED!" Naeem continued. "I do not think going back in there is a good idea. And . . . " Naeem shifted as if he was uncomfortable and hesitated.

"And what?' Suzi asked.

"Well…" Naeem continued to hesitate.

"Dude, what's wrong? Just say it," Tyler encouraged.

Naeem signed, "That man . . . the one from the cave . . . he recognized you two." He nodded at Suzi and Tyler.

"Recognized us? How so?' Suzi asked.

"All I remember is that he said he knew your grandfather," Naeem replied.

Suzi looked at Tyler, "Well, that explains why he looks so familiar. You were right; he must have been in one of Grampa's old photos."

"Suz, we gotta go back in there. We need answers. *I* want answers." Tyler looked at his sister.

"So do I," she replied.

Naeem raised his hand, "Uh . . . let me remind you all, they mentioned *bloodshed*. Are we sure we are not getting over our heads here?"

"I know it's risky, but we won't exactly get answers any other way," Emma commented.

"She's right." Ty looked at his friend and took note of Naeem's serious reservations about heading back into the cave. "It'll be okay, Naeem. I got your back." Ty placed his hand on Naeem's shoulder.

Still not convinced, Naeem stared at the others for a moment and conceded. "Fine, but if I die in there, Papa is going to kill me."

"Perfect. It's on then. Let's meet at the research tent just before dawn," Suzi declared.

"Before dawn?" Tyler exclaimed. "What the heck? Why so friggin' early? I need my beauty sleep!"

"Yeah, well, sleep isn't going to help whatever is going on with all this." Suzi waved her hand around in the direction of her brother. She ignored the frown aimed directly at her. "But we need to get out of camp before anyone wakes up. The diggers usually start prepping at sunrise. If they catch us, they will alert our parents, and we won't be going anywhere. Hopefully, we can get back before breakfast, and no one will even notice we're gone."

With that, the four of them agreed to meet near the research tent at 4:30 a.m., and each set their phone alarms.

19

Music blared from Ty's alarm in the Carruth tent at 4 a.m. Ty quickly reached to shut it off before it woke his mom. Ellie stirred, but only for a moment. Suzi, on the other hand, jumped straight up. Once they were sure their mom was back to sleep, they dressed quickly and quietly, then grabbed their backpacks and flashlights and left the tent.

"Oh wait!" Ty stopped and ran back inside. Moments later, he came out, stuffing a handful of neon green rods into his backpack.

"What are those?" Suzi hissed.

"Glow sticks. I brought them from home to use around the campfires, but I thought this might be a better time to use them," Ty replied.

"Ooooookay. Why?" Suzi asked.

"Because last time, your flashlight died," Ty answered, with a tone of sarcasm, as he walked past his sister.

"Oh. Right. Good thinking," Suzi agreed and followed behind him.

Emma arrived at the research tent first. Suzi and Tyler arrived shortly after, and Naeem walked up moments later.

"Hey, guys. You ready?" Suzi asked quietly.

Naeem whispered back. "I guess so, but if my father finds out, I will be in so much trouble!" He wanted to make sure he got one last protest in before they left.

"Me too!" Emma agreed while having second thoughts.

But Suzi wasn't fazed. "We'll *all* be in trouble if we get caught. So let's not get caught, shall we? Everybody have your flashlights?" Suzi asked. The four of them lit their flashlights, and Suzi led the way out of camp.

From the campsite, it was less than a ten-minute walk to the cave entrance. The kids, even Suzi, were unusually quiet on the walk.

As they approached the cave's opening, Emma said, "I have a bad feeling about this."

Naeem agreed. "Maybe we should go back."

Suzi and Ty both looked back at Naeem. Noticing their stare, he reluctantly agreed. "Okay, fine. Just go!"

Emma took a quick glance back toward camp and noticed a flashlight roaming around the camp. "Hey! Psst!" as she motioned the others to return. "Is the crew usually up at this hour?"

The other three poked their heads out of the cave entrance. "Turn your flashlights off!" Suzi said quickly. The others did as she asked, then stared back at camp.

"Sometimes Nora gets up early to get a head start on pulling tools for the day," Naeem recalled quietly.

"*This* early?" Emma whispered back.

"Not usually. But I guess it is possible." Naeem continued, "Wait, you don't think it's . . . those bad men?"

"Nah, it's just the crew," Suzi replied, but she wasn't sure if she was trying to reassure the others, or herself.

As they all stepped back into the cave, Suzi gave another concerned glance out towards camp.

They turned their flashlights back on and moved slowly through the main hallway toward the maze of turns that led to the area they had been in only days ago. After maneuvering through the hallways for about fifteen minutes, suddenly, their flashlights flickered and dimmed. Then, one by one, all four lights died completely.

"Ummm . . . Suz?" Ty exclaimed, shaking his flashlight.

"What the heck? Get those glow sticks," Suzi replied, shaking her flashlight to try to figure out why it had died.

While Tyler was digging around his backpack in the dark for four glow sticks, Naeem asked, "Does anyone else feel weird?"

"Yeah, like the hair on the back of my neck is standing straight up. It's really creepy!" Emma went on. "Something is giving me the heebeegeebees!"

"The heeba-what?" Tyler asked as he handed a glow stick to each of them.

"It's just a phrase my Mum used when she was really creeped out about something." Emma continued, "How do you make this glow thing work?"

"Bend and shake it," Suzi replied.

"Ah! Got it!" Emma continued, "I am absolutely freezing!"

All four of them shivered. "Yeah, me too!" Suzi continued. "Definitely much colder than I remember, and I agree. It's a whole lot creepier this time!"

"Emma, I have an extra jacket in my bag." Naeem quickly knelt down and pulled the jacket from his bag. Tyler stared at his friend with a suspicious grin. "What? She's cold!"

"Uh huh," Ty snickered.

Naeem walked over to Emma and handed her his jacket. "Thanks!" she said.

Ty whispered to Suzi. "Don't you think it's weird that all four flashlights died at the same time?"

"Yeah, totally weird, but let's just keep going. I know we're getting close," she replied.

They took a few steps forward. "Ugh! Gross! What is that

smell?" Emma exclaimed.

"Oh, yuck! Nasty!" Tyler responded, then stopped. "Wait, do you hear that?"

"Hear what . . . ?" Suzi started, when all four of them stopped dead in their tracks.

The air in the cavern had become even colder, the horrible smell became stronger, and suddenly, a ghostly figure appeared from around the corner, only ten feet away from them. Frozen and completely unable to speak, all four kids stared at the beautiful figure in front of them. She had a long, sleek body and a subtle glowing aura around her. Black eyeliner carved out her deep brown eyes, which were set behind sharp, elegant cheekbones. Her tawny skin was flawless, even through the ghostly mist. She was simply beautiful. A tall gold headpiece and a beautiful gold and blue necklace hinted at her status. Although the figure moved with regal gracefulness, she seemed upset. She wept and paced back and forth while rubbing her wrist as if she was worried or had lost something.

Still frozen with fear, the four of them continued to stare at the figure hovering before them.

Tyler broke the silence. "Suuuuzz?"

"Yeeeah."

"Please tell me you see that."

"Yep, I see that."

Emma looked over at Naeem, whose olive skin had taken on a rather pale shade of white. "Are you okay?" she asked, but Naeem continued to stare and gave an affirmative nod.

Emma then turned back to the figure. "Who, or what is that?"

Standing perfectly still and in utter shock, Suzi replied breathlessly. "Hoooly Mother of Goodness . . . if I'm not mistaken . . . I think that's Nefertiti." Suzi could not believe her eyes!

And as if all three had just snapped out of some trance, they whipped their heads around to Suzi.

"What?!" Ty exclaimed.

"Shhh! Don't scare her away!" Suzi continued. "And you heard me. Seriously, I think this is Nefertiti."

"THE Nefertiti?" Naeem questioned.

"Yep," Suzi whispered but continued to stand perfectly still. She stared at this amazing sight. She could not believe what she was seeing.

"What should we do?" Emma asked quietly.

"How should I know?" Suzi replied.

"Because! You are YOU!" Naeem retorted.

"Shhh! What's that supposed to mean?" Suzi snapped back in a hard whisper.

They all looked back at her in disbelief, but before they could respond, a huge whirl of wind and sand whipped through the hallway, stinging their skin. The figure was gone.

"Wait! Where did she go?" Naeem exclaimed.

Suddenly, as if someone had flipped on a switch, all four flashlights turned on again.

"Woah! What the heck?" Tyler looked over his flashlight in disbelief.

With a deep breath, Suzi said, "We must be close! Let's keep moving." Excited, her eyes lit up. She gave a big toothy grin and motioned everyone to follow her. Suzi only got about five feet when she realized the others were not behind her. "Well, come on!" she said.

Naeem pushed the other two forward. "You too!" Suzi waved to Naeem. Reluctantly, he followed behind them, wide-eyed and visibly shaken.

Suzi pulled a piece of paper from her pocket and asked herself which direction to go next.

"What's that you've got there?" Emma pointed her flashlight on the paper.

"It's just some notes I jotted down from our last time here," Suzi replied.

A few minutes later, Suzi noticed that she could no longer hear the others' footsteps. Nor did she hear any of their complaints about it being dark or whether she knew where she was going. Suzi turned to look behind her. She saw the three of them standing perfectly still.

"What? Another ghost? What are you waiting . . . " She noticed they looked even more frightened than before. She raised her flashlight a little higher and saw two men standing behind them with their hands on Tyler and Naeem's shoulders.

Suzi recognized one man right away. He was the man they had seen last week, and she realized Ty was right. He was definitely the man from one of Grampa's photographs.

"Well, well. What have we here? 'Ello there, lil' miss!" the older man said. "I remember you. You're one of ole Collin Carruth's kids."

"Grandkids . . . and what do you want?" Suzi glared as she responded. The others stood perfectly still. But Suzi seemed more agitated than scared.

"I want the bracelet," the old man said.

"What bracelet?" Suzi answered sarcastically.

Angry at her response, the Frenchman demanded. "The bracelet that was taken!"

"Easy there, mate." He waved off the Frenchman. "We'll get it from them one way or another." The older man continued, "Besides, this lot might lead us to more than just the bracelet." The old Englishman then pointed his gun at Suzi. "Now . . . where were you lot 'eading off to?"

"We don't know about any bracelet!" Tyler defiantly spoke

up.

The old man turned to Tyler. "I know you too. You're one of Collin's kids as well."

"Geez, dude! Grandkids! *GRAND*-kids! Don't you listen!?" Suzi retorted.

"Whatever you are, you are getting on my nerves!" the Frenchman growled.

"Do I care?" Suzi responded angrily.

"I care, Suz. I care," Naeem said, fearfully.

Suzi looked at Naeem, then at Emma and Tyler. She quickly realized her every word could have serious consequences when she noticed the gun pointed toward Naeem.

"Fine," Suzi growled. "We were heading in this direction."

"There, that's a good lass. Now, lead the way." The old man then pointed his gun at her and directed her to move forward. "We want that bracelet."

"We already told you, we don't know anything about any bracelet. We've just been in here exploring," Suzi said.

"Right . . . *exploring*. At this time of the mornin'? Now keep movin,'" the old man demanded.

At 5 a.m., the early morning sun began to creep over the horizon, and the camp rumbled with the sounds of an early start to another productive day. Ellie and Mundi stood near the worktable just outside of the research tent discussing plans for the day. Ellie decided it would be best not to revisit the mysterious conversation they had the other night. She wanted to continue forward with the progress they'd made in the last day or so. They had stalled enough, and she didn't want to disrupt the positive direction of the project.

A moment later, Asim walked up, clearly worried. "Have you seen Emma? I cannot find her."

"I noticed that my kids were up and about really early this morning too. I'm sure she and Suzi are just having some breakfast. Did you look in the mess tent?" Ellie replied.

"Yes, yes. She is not there. I looked all over. I woke up, and she was already gone. She never leaves our sleeping quarters in the morning without telling me she is leaving!"

At that moment, Ahmal approached the group from behind and asked, "Good morning, all. Has anyone seen that silly boy of mine? We have work to do."

"Naeem is missing too?" Asim asked anxiously.

"Missing?" Ahmal continued. "Who is missing? And what do you mean 'too'?"

"My Emma! I cannot find her!"

"Come to think of it, I haven't seen either of mine this morning. Since they were up before me, I just figured they'd gone to grab an early breakfast."

"Aunt Ellie!" Jake came running up. "Oh, hey guys," he quickly addressed the others. "Aunt Ellie, some of the workers said they saw outsiders in the camp again this morning. They ran them off but said that they didn't look like vagrants. Rashidi said he thought they might be treasure hunters."

"Allah, have mercy!" Ahmal cried out.

"Wait. What's going on?" Jake asked as he noticed the frightened look on everyone's face.

Asim replied, "The kids are missing. All four of them!" Asim then looked squarely at Mandi. "Mandisa, it is time!"

"Time for what? For goodness sake! Would one of you please tell me what is going on? Where are the kids?" Ellie demanded as she looked at Mandi and Asim.

Mandi said, "Come inside." She opened the flap of the tent. Ellie, Asim, Ahmal, and Jake followed her inside.

"Sit, please, sit," Mandi motioned.

"I do not want to sit! Where is my son?!" Ahmal was worried and frustrated.

Asim put his hand on Ahmal's shoulder. "My friend, we *will* find your son, but for now, please sit."

Reluctantly, Ahmal took a seat on the stool next to Asim.

Mandi picked up her cell phone and dialed. Mandi began to speak on the phone in both English and Arabic. "Father, it is time. We have to tell the others. Yes, I know, but the children are missing, and the Network has been spotted in camp." After a moment, she continued, "I trust Ellie. And Asim assures me that the others can be trusted as well." Mandi continued, "We will be careful. I promise. I will call you soon. Ma 'a al-sssalāmah Father (Peace be with you)." Mandi hung up her phone and sent out a text message.

"What was all that about?" Ahmal insisted.

"Uh, what is going on?" Jake added.

Ellie looked cautiously at her friend. Over the last couple of weeks, she knew something was up. Mandi seemed overly distracted and defensive regarding this project, which was unlike her. Mandi was tough, smart, and one of the best Egyptologists any of them had ever worked with. However, Ellie was both worried and oddly relieved that her old friend trusted her. "Okay, all this is making me nervous. Do you know where the kids are?" Ellie asked.

Just as Mandi was about to speak, Nora and two members of the digging crew stepped inside the tent and stood in front of the door. Two more men appeared to be standing guard outside.

"Okay, now it's official! I'm definitely nervous. Where are the kids?!" Ellie demanded.

Asim gave Mandi a quick nod.

Mandi sighed, "Are you all familiar with an ancient society

called the Medjay?"

"The Medjay?" Ahmal responded. "You mean . . . *the* Medjay, the ancient guardians of the Pharaohs of Egypt . . . that Medjay?"

"Yes, Ahmal, *that* Medjay," Asim answered.

"There has been no mention of them since the 12th Dynasty. What do they have to do with my missing son?" Ahmal exclaimed.

"Ahmal, please try to calm down. We will locate the children, I promise. But right now, we need to fill you in on a serious matter that might help us," Asim reassured his friend. Jake, Ahmal, and Ellie sat and listened as Mandi and Asim started from the beginning.

20

1300s BC—18th Dynasty—Akhenaten (The Heretic King) (Legend of the Queen)

Due to the death of her favorite daughter, Princess Meketaten, Nefertiti, the royal wife of the pharaoh Akhenaten, began to have second thoughts regarding the changes in Egypt's religion. It was said that Akhenaten was angered by this deception and banished Nefertiti from The City of Akhenaten. No proof of this deception actually existed. Legend said, however, that once Nefertiti was cast out, the priests, who Akhenaten had also forced to change religions, feared for the Queen's life and took her in. They hid her with the secret Medjay so Akhenaten could never find her. Distraught over being cast out and the loss of her daughter, Nefertiti eventually died from heartbreak and despair. Her favorite possessions were the gold and lapis necklace and bracelet that once belonged to her beloved daughter, Meketaten. As such, the priest and Medjay buried these items with her, so that her daughter would be with her in the afterlife. However, the priests were afraid that he would try to find her once Akhenaten heard of her death. Then, out of rage and revenge, he might desecrate the tomb and eliminate her from her peaceful afterlife. With these thoughts in mind, the priests cursed the bracelet and necklace in hopes that if the pharaoh indeed found her, he and his followers would be cursed with disease and devastation forever. The curse would be reversed, however, if the bracelet or the necklace were returned to Nefertiti and the tomb left intact by the sixth full moon. The Medjay vowed to protect her, even in death, as they protected all the pharaohs of Egypt. Even though there was no evidence of the Medjay's existence since the 12th Dynasty, it was said that they continued to protect Egypt in secrecy throughout the centuries and that their ancestral legacies exist even in the modern day.

Six months ago, the Valley of the Queens

A family of Bedouin shepherds sought shelter from a terrible sandstorm in a nearby cave. A curious young boy began wandering around the cave passages when he happened upon an object wrapped in a tattered linen cloth. The object seemed to be lodged between the wall and the floor. He pulled on the object, but it simply would not budge. He tried pushing the wall, pulling the cloth harder, but again, it would not budge. The young boy took a small piece of wood from his shoulder bag and began to dig around the object until, finally, he was able to pull it free. The object itself was released, but a small piece of the ancient fabric was left behind. What he held in his trembling hands left him breathless. A pouch of such beauty, he didn't dare open it. He quickly ran back to his family with his prize. "Mama! Baba, look! Look what I found!"

The boy's grandfather quickly leaped to his feet. "Do not open that! Did you open it? Did you touch anything inside?"

"No, Gedo. I did not!" the boy replied and handed the pouch to his grandfather. "I found it in a corridor around the corner."

His grandfather gently took the pouch and gazed at its magnificence. He opened the pouch but was careful not to touch its contents. As he pulled the pouch away from the delicate object inside, a stunning gold and lapis bracelet was revealed, the likes of which he had never seen. The family gathered around the elder and stared at the beautiful object.

"What is it, Gedo?" the boy asked. "What is it?"

"My son, I think this treasure belonged to someone very special."

"How do you know, Gedo?"

"See this?" The elder pointed to the hieroglyphics encrusted on the outside of the pouch. "This tells of a Queen who once ruled over the city of Akhenaten!"

"The city of Akhenaten? Where is this city?" the boy asked.

"Sadiki, my boy, we really must get you more books to read. I do not like how little you know about our history," the elder said.

The boy's father smiled and explained. "My son, the city of Akhenaten was the ancient city where Pharaoh Akhenaten, 'the heretic king,' ruled."

"Can you show me where you found this?" the elder asked.

"Yes, Gedo," Sadiki said. "It is this way; follow me!"

His grandfather and parents grabbed a few torches and followed him deep into the cave. After about ten minutes, his mother remarked, "Sadiki! You came this far into the cave without permission?"

The boy turned to look at his mother with a mischievous smile. "I am sorry, Mama. It is just around the next corner." A moment later, "It was there. See Gedo. There!" The boy pointed to the ragged fabric still wedged between the wall and floor of the cave.

"Here?" his father said. "But this is a wall!" Sadiki's mother knelt next to him. "Are you sure, my son? There is no door here; it is nothing but a wall."

"Yes, see this fabric? It was wrapped in this fabric." Sadiki pointed.

"How did you remove the pouch?" Gedo asked.

"I dug it out with this." The boy pulled the small piece of wood from his pocket.

Sadiki began to show them how he dug out the object when a huge burst of swirling sand appeared and blasted them. They fell to the floor and tried to cover their bodies from the stinging sand. "Stay down!" Gedo yelled. But they could barely hear him. The noise from the wind was so loud.

"What is going on?" The father yelled as he reached to cover his son with the side of his jacket. Sadiki's mother crawled close to her husband, and he held her tight. As the wind and sand continued to whirl around them, they could hear what seemed to be a woman crying. Then, as quickly as it started, it stopped.

Stunned, Gedo grabbed his grandson. "Are you okay?"

"Yes." Sadiki brushed the sand from his parents. "Mama! Baba! Are you okay?"

Extremely shaken, his mother replied, "Yes, I think so. What on earth was that?" Sadiki helped his mother stand.

His grandfather said, "I do not know, but I believe it is time for us to leave."

They all agreed. Unfortunately, the sand and wind ruined the torches they brought with them. They were forced to rely on a few matches Sadiki's father had in his shoulder bag to guide them through the corridors to their camp near the cave entrance.

At sunrise, the Bedouin family packed up their belongings and left the cave. Still in their possession was the purple pouch that contained the bracelet young Sadiki had found.

As the Bedouin family finished dinner and prepared their flock to bed for the evening, a sudden ruckus came from the other end of camp. A small girl ran screaming from the far side of camp to her mother, who had been cleaning up after dinner.

Sadiki quickly ran over to his aunt and little cousin. "What is happening?"

"I do not know!" his aunt replied. "Quick! Take Kami and go inside the tent."

Sadiki did as he was told. He ran into the tent and hid his little cousin under a stack of blankets. He pulled back the tent flap enough to see that a group of desert pirates had invaded their peaceful camp. These outlaws were there to steal food and supplies. His family fought back, but the pirates outnumbered them and ransacked every tent. As they approached Sadiki's tent, he quickly hid under the blankets with his cousin.

Once inside, the men tossed everything onto the floor and were just about to uncover Sadiki and Kami's hiding spot when a man from outside yelled in and said. "This is enough. It is time to go. Bashir has found something."

Sadiki panicked because he knew immediately what they had found. As soon as it was safe, he rushed out of hiding and ran towards his grandfather's tent. What he saw made him sick. His mother was tending to a cut on his grandfather's head. He had taken quite a knock to the head when he tried to stop the thieves. On the ground lay his uncle. Sadiki's father and aunt were desperately trying to save him.

"Is Gedo going to be alright?" Sadiki asked his mother as he handed her a fresh cloth.

"Yes, I believe so," she replied.

"What about Uncle Manu?" Sadiki's voice trembled because he knew it did not look good.

"I do not know. Your father is trying to save him. They beat him very badly."

Just then, little Kami ran up, but Sadiki grabbed his cousin and held her close while the family worked to save her father, Manu. After a while, it looked like their efforts were enough, and Sadiki's Uncle Manu would survive the vicious attack.

Sadiki walked over to his grandfather. "They stole the pouch, didn't they?"

"Yes."

"What will happen now?" Sadiki asked sadly.

"I do not know. But after what happened to us in the cave that day, I fear these men do not realize what they have. They think they have a prize. They do not understand. It could be dangerous!"

Another month later . . .
Western Europe Antiquities Network—Headquarters.
Paris, France

Hidden in a flat on Quai du Louvre Street, just two blocks from the Louvre Museum in Paris, was the home and office of Malcolm Maldroon. Maldroon was one of the world's most infamous black-market antiquities dealers. He ran a network of operatives that sought out some of the world's most rare and beautiful artifacts. Many of these items were then sold on the black market for millions of dollars. Maldroon was Scottish-born but left Scotland to work as an apprentice for renowned American archaeologist Collinsworth Carruth. It became apparent to Collin Carruth that Malcolm's intentions had quickly turned from science to financial gain after he introduced young Malcolm to a small group of treasure seekers he knew through mutual friends. Collin Carruth knew many people on both sides of the antiquities community and was often sought out by enterprising individuals as a source of merchandise. Although Collin had a questionable side, he usually did the right thing and turned most of his findings over to the local authorities or museums. But this did not stop those with less than honorable intentions from seeking him out. Malcolm voiced his frustrations with Collin's decisions many times. And as a result, Collin had to fire Malcolm. This led to a great deal of animosity between the two. The feud also led to Malcolm's rise in the world of black market antiquities.

Malcolm sat on his top-floor veranda, enjoying a beautiful sunset and a crisp martini. The city skyline was beautiful that time of day. He watched as tour boats trolled up and down the Seine River and through the heart of Paris. A hard knock on the door disturbed his quiet, pensive moment. Malcolm took one last look at the evening lights of the city before answering the door.

"It's about time. What took you two so long? I called for you hours ago," Malcolm growled.

"We're sorry, Mr. Maldroon, sir. Traffic," the older man said, as the two men stepped inside the beautiful flat and waited to be invited to sit.

"Well, sit down." Malcolm continued, "We've got a lot to discuss."

The two men anxiously sat in two chairs across from their boss. Remy Cobb pulled a large envelope from his briefcase and handed it to Malcolm. "This is the information you requested on the value of the industry's most recent item."

Malcolm opened the envelope and shuffled through its contents. "Exactly how did this item suddenly find itself available?" he asked.

"A small clan of shepherds found it in a cave inside the Valley of the Queens." He continued, "But they were robbed one night by a band of thieves."

"Let me guess, these thieves decided to make a few bucks and sell it at a street market somewhere," Malcolm interrupted.

"Yes, and the person who bought it was that washed-up old archaeologist, Nicholas McIntyre," Remy said.

"Does he still have it?" Malcolm asked.

"Yes."

"Well, I guess we need to offer to buy it from him." Malcolm placed his Martini glass on the table, crossed his legs, and picked up the computer tablet resting on the table next to him. "Let's see, what can we offer? Hmmm."

"Beggin' your pardon, Sir, but I've tried. He won't part wiff' it. He's determined to hold on to it," Remy said, reluctantly.

"And why is that?" Malcolm questioned.

"Because he wants to make sure it goes to the Cairo Museum," Remy replied.

"Oh, dear Lord. Another idiot with principles." Malcolm continued, "Alright then. André, I believe this is in your area of expertise. I'm sure you can find a way to persuade him." Malcolm turned to André Gagnon, his French bodyguard and, at times, enforcer.

"Yes, I believe I can encourage him to see the value in selling the artifact to us," André replied.

"Good. It's settled then. That piece is worth over five million dollars. I want it on our market board as soon as possible." Maldroon stood and said, "I'm sure you two can see yourselves out."

A few days later
Portobello Market—London, England

A mysteriously beautiful woman sat at a sidewalk café, while the morning was disturbed by the murder of a man at the local antique shop across the street. She watched as the assailant fled the area and ran into the Inn, located just above the café, where she had been having her morning tea. She walked around the area all day, keeping an eye on the Inn, waiting for the assailant to venture out. Finally, around 6:00 p.m., the man came to the café for dinner. She watched his every move and eventually conversed with her target.

"A handsome man such as yourself shouldn't be here all alone." She was stunningly attractive. Her cobalt blue eyes mesmerized him as he turned to face her. She stroked his arm and asked, "Can I buy you a drink?"

"Yes, that would be nice," he replied in a thick French accent that she could hardly understand, which was horrible, given that she spoke French fluently.

"Perfect!" She stepped up and asked the barkeeper to mix the man whatever drink he wanted.

The barkeeper and the woman both turned to look at him. "What would you like, Sir," the barkeeper asked. "Gin, s'il vous plait," the man requested.

"Gin it is," the barkeeper replied.

The woman discreetly slid her hand into the side of her small purse. The barkeeper placed the glass of gin on the bar and walked away. She discreetly released a small white pill into the glass from the palm of her hand, as she politely picked up the glass and handed it to the Frenchman. The pill had dissolved instantly. The Frenchman took the glass and enjoyed his first sip.

The two exchanged small talk for a few moments. But soon, the Frenchman decided he was extremely tired and wanted to retire for the evening. He thanked the woman for the drink and walked to the stairs leading to the second floor of the Inn. A bit unsteady, he carefully made his way up the stairs. The woman tipped the barkeeper, picked up her purse, and silently followed her target.

Once upstairs, she stood in front of the door to the Frenchman's room and pulled a small leather pouch from her purse. She pulled two tiny tools from the pouch and began to pick the lock on the door. Quietly, she entered the room and closed the door. There, lying face down on the bed, was the man she'd watched all day, drugged only moments ago. She stood over him for a few minutes to make certain he was completely asleep. He was definitely out cold. She rifled through the furniture and his belongings. When she looked under the bed, she found a silver briefcase. Quietly, she slid the case from beneath the bed. Once again, she pulled the small pouch from her purse and picked the lock on the briefcase. She opened the case, and there it was. Her mission to retrieve the valuable artifact was complete. She quietly closed the case. Then, with the case in hand, she swiftly descended the stairs. Completely unnoticed, she slipped out the back door of the Inn. Once in the back alley, she pulled a cell phone from her purse.

"Yes, good evening. I'd like to book a one-way flight to Casablanca for tonight. First Class, please. Thank you."

21

"Okay, so, let me get this straight. You, your father, and Asim, along with apparently several members of this crew," Jake looked around, "are part of this ancient society?"

"Keepers of Egypt," Asim interrupted.

Jake looked at Asim. "Ooookay, these 'Keepers of Egypt,' aaand this blood antiquities network is *here*, hunting for a trinket that *you* apparently have." He, again, looked over to Mandi. "And the kids are missing."

Mandi and Asim gave an affirmative nod. Jake, Ellie, and Ahmal stared at Mandi wide-eyed. They simply couldn't believe what they had just heard. "Okay, so, where is this bracelet?" Ellie asked.

Mandi went to her trunk and pulled out a small plain wooden box. She opened the box and pulled out a beautiful purple linen pouch. Carefully, she opened the pouch and revealed a beautiful gold and lapis bracelet.

"By the way you're handling that thing, I assume it's cursed," Jake mentioned.

"Yes, unfortunately, that is the myth," Mandi admitted.

Ahmal finally broke his silence. "Okay, we have what they want. Can we trade the bracelet for the kids?"

Mandi hung her head low and sighed. She did not want to disappoint Ahmal.

Ellie noticed Mandi's reaction. "Ahmal, I have a feeling it isn't that simple."

"No, I'm afraid it's not," Mandi agreed. "We only have until sunset tomorrow to return it to Nefertiti's tomb."

Ellie stood up, rubbed her face, then looked at Mandi. "Okay, well, we have to get the kids back. That's the priority."

"Most certainly!" Ahmal declared as he stood up next to Ellie.

"Trust me! We *will* get them back." Ellie placed her hand on Ahmal's shoulder. She was worried too, very worried. The kids had run off to explore, but never this long and never without someone having seen them at some point during the day.

"I may actually know where they went," Mandi suggested. "Given the need for protection and secrecy with it all, I've tried to watch the comings and goings around camp. And I believe a cave entrance is in the hills next to camp. I've seen them coming out of there a few times. They've been very secretive lately, huddling together and whispering. Ellie, I think they may have actually found a grave site."

"A grave site?" Ellie looked at Mandi. " Or *the* grave site?"

"She's in those hills, isn't she?" Jake stood straight up and looked at Mandi. "I was right all along!"

Ahmal interrupted, "Not the time, my friend, but *definitely* later."

"Yes, Jake. You were, as you always are, absolutely correct. And I'm sorry for the problems it caused," Mandi apologized. "I will explain more later, but right now, I think we need to get into that cave."

"Okay, do we know where to begin looking?" Ellie asked.

"Well, Jake's calculations and maps seem to be spot on," Mandi continued, as she looked at the map laid out on the table. "And I have seen them coming out of a cave on the north side of one of the large hills here . . . " She said, pointing to a spot on the map.

Nora chimed in, "I've also seen them climbing out of a large hole about eight feet up from a ledge on the same hill. It's only about a few hundred yards outside of camp."

"Alright, we know they've been in there more than once, obviously, so it stands to reason they'd go back. And, if Suzi thinks for one second the grave is in there, you can bet that's where they've gone," Ellie continued. "Let's grab our bags and meet at the edge of camp in five minutes!"

They quickly split up. Moments later, Ellie, Mandi, Ahmal, Asim, Jake, and Nora all met at the edge of camp. "I say we go in through the north end. It'll be faster than all of us trying to climb up the side of that hill," Ellie declared. The team agreed, and off they went.

On the short walk to the cliffs along the north edge, Mandi pulled out her phone and began texting. Ellie walked over. "Please, no more secrets."

"I'm just texting my father. I need to tell him what is going on and to make sure we have backup."

"You think we need backup?" said Ellie, with a tone of concern.

"Hopefully not, but with this antiquities network, one never knows," Mandi replied.

Once at the base of the cliff, they quickly climbed up to the ledge near the opening of a cave. "This is where I have seen them go in and out of," Mandi acknowledged.

"Okay, let's go in and find them." Ahmal pushed through the group to the cave entrance.

"Wait, Ahmal. You and Nora need to be out here guarding the entrance," Mandi advised.

"No! I need to go find my son! I cannot sit out here and wait. What if you need my help in there!" he exclaimed.

"I understand, but we need you two to make sure we don't

have any surprise visitors while we're inside," Mandi continued. "And my father has seen to it that we will have all the assistance we may need."

Asim motioned to the others, "Let's go."

Ahmal looked devastated and helpless as he watched the others enter the cave without him. Nora placed her hand on her old friend's arm. "This is where we are needed most right now. By protecting this entrance, we ensure the balance stays in our favor inside that cave. They will bring Naeem out of there. I have no doubt."

Ahmal reluctantly agreed.

Jake looked back. "We will find him. I promise."

22

"Hey, kid! You! The skinny one, hand me that bag!" Remy pointed to the backpack that Naeem dropped, when he realized that they were not alone in the corridor. Naeem picked up the bag and handed it to the man, but casually dropped his glow stick onto the ground.

"Now get moving!" Remy demanded.

Suzi led them down the corridor, then turned left and continued toward the middle of the cave. Suzi wanted so badly to hit one of them with her backpack and run, but she knew if she made any slight move, her brother, Naeem, and Emma could all be in danger.

"Collin told me you're the smart one, said you'd probably end up at Oxford like y'ur dear ole Mum and Dad," Remy said to Suzi.

"I don't know what you're talking about. My brother is pretty smart; maybe he meant him." Suzi was so angry she could hardly contain her sarcasm.

"Keep me out of this, Suz," Ty whispered.

"No, it's you. His granddaughter. He was right proud'a boaf' yous, actually. Said so the day he died."

Suzi whipped around and flashed her flashlight at Remy. "What do you know about my grandfather's death?" Suzi was as fired up as she had ever been in her entire life. "You weren't there!"

"Yes, poppet, I was." Remy walked toward Suzi. She began to walk backward slowly. "That's right. I was there on the plane . . . that day. Barely made out wiff' me life."

"Why? Why were *you* there?" Suzi was insistent.

Ty stepped forward. "He's lying, Suz, there's no way Grampa would've had anything to do with this guy, nor would Dad!"

"We had business together in South America, al'right. Maybe y'ur ole' granddad was into more than you thought, ehh!" Remy insisted as he flashed his flashlight forward. "Now keep moving!"

André pushed Emma forward, which made her trip and fall.

"Hey! Watch it!" Naeem jumped over to help her up, glaring at the Frenchman as if he could punch him.

"Just move!" André waved his gun at the kids.

"Look, all we found was a hole in a wall. We don't actually know where any treasure is," Emma told Remy.

"You lot have been in here several times now. Don't be' telling me you don't know where it is," Remy continued. "Otherwise, you wouldn't be in here now."

"What exactly are you looking for?" Suzi asked.

"Well, to start, we want the bracelet that was stolen from ole André here," Remy declared, then continued. "Then, we want whatever other treasures you found in here."

Suzi took a step toward Remy, "We already told you, we don't know about any bracelet. And we haven't stumbled across any treasure in here either. Like Emma said, all we've found is A HOLE IN THE WALL!" By this point, Suzi was running out of patience.

"Alright then. Let's see this bloomin' hole. How big is it?" Remy asked.

"Only about eight or so inches wide, and I have no idea if I can even find it again," Suzi replied.

"You better 'ope you can," Remy insisted and pointed his

gun at her.

Suzi rolled her eyes in a way that only a fourteen-year-old girl could and sighed. "Fine." Then she turned toward the area where they had seen the hole. "This way."

André and Remy followed the kids as they made their way through the cave's passages. A few minutes into their trek through the maze, they heard a scuff in the distance.

"What was that?" André asked as he moved his flashlight around.

"Probably just a rat or som'em," Remy replied.

Not convinced, André reluctantly pushed the kids forward.

It wasn't long before they came to the wall where they had found the hole.

"It's here. Now, let us go!" Suzi pointed to the small hole in the wall.

"Go?" Remy asked. "Oh, I can't do that, miss."

"Why not!" Emma asked, frustrated.

"Because you've seen ole André and me'self. I think we'll have to take you back wiff' us." Remy got really close to Suzi's face.

Suzi wasn't having any of it. She was angry, frustrated, and fed up. "You need a Tic Tac!" Suzi frowned and stood her ground.

"Look here, poppet, I've 'ad 'bout 'nough of you," Remy growled.

Suddenly, with a quick flash, something moved in the shadows.

"What was that?" André jumped slightly and shined his flashlight in the corner to see what was there.

"What was what?" Remy demanded.

"I just saw something . . . over there!" André continued to point his flashlight in the direction of the shadow that caught his attention.

"You idiot. Now you're seeing things," Remy replied, shaking his head.

Just then, as if out of nowhere, Mandi appeared from behind them with ninja skills like nothing the kids had ever seen. She pounced on Remy with the precision of a well-trained and skilled fighter. She blocked his weapon and threw a quick kick to his stomach and an elbow chop to the neck. Remy was down in an instant.

Stunned, the kids flattened themselves against the cave wall and watched as Mandi swiftly disarmed and subdued Remy. Her martial arts skills were no match for him.

During the scuffle, André tried to see through the dimly lit hallway. He lifted his gun to fire, but from the shadows, another man, dressed in all black, appeared and moved like an assassin on a mission. The man took André from behind, placing his arm around his neck. André fought his attacker hard. But the man's rapid and fluid movements were overwhelming. A second man appeared and gave a well-placed high kick to Andre's face, and the first man quickly swept André's legs out from under him. In mere seconds, André, too, had been disarmed and laid face down on the ground.

Within only minutes, Mandi and her two Medjay friends felt they had the situation firmly under control.

Suddenly, Remy decided to move towards his gun. But one of Mandi's friends stepped over, forcing him back to the ground with his foot. "I do not think that is a good idea." He then reached down, grabbed the gun, and pointed it at Remy.

All four kids stood wide-eyed and motionless as they watched Mandi and her associates tying up Remy and André.

"Suz, your godmother is some kinda freakin' Ninja!" Ty broke the silence with a declaration of amazement.

Just then, Ellie and Asim burst into the cavern, breathless from running, followed quickly by Jake, breathing heavily from a sprint.

"Papa!" Emma yelled. Asim ran to his daughter and gave her a giant bear hug.

"Oh, my Emma!" Asim hugged her so hard Emma could barely breathe.

"Not breathing, Papa."

Asim released his daughter. "Are you okay? Why did you leave without telling me? You are in a lot of trouble, young lady!"

Ellie stood at the entrance of the corridor, breathing heavily. She stared at Suzi and Ty. She was so angry she could barely speak. But, at the same time, her relief that they were okay nearly brought her to tears. "I am so angry with you two! What on Earth made you think going off on your own like this was okay?!"

"I'm sorry, Mom," Suzi apologized. She knew full well her mom was really angry.

"Me too." Tyler echoed his sister's apology. "We just wanted to find out what was in this hole."

"Dr. Carruth, it was all my fault." Naeem stepped up. "I am the one who suggested we go to the cave to explore in the first place."

"That's no excuse!" Ellie scolded. "How many times have I told you guys NOT to venture out on your own? Do you have any idea how close you came to being killed?! I am just so unbelievably angry with you two!"

While the kids were taking their tongue-lashing, Jake walked over to look at the hole the kids felt was so important to investigate. He flashed his flashlight into the hole, then poked his eye up next to the hole and looked inside. "Aunt Ellie, take a look at this."

Ellie glared back at Suzi and Tyler one more time for good measure, then stepped over to see what was so important that they'd risk going into the cave alone. Ellie placed her head next to the hole.

"Do you see what I see?" Jake asked her. Ellie pulled her head back quickly, "Is that . . . ?"

"I think so!" Jake quickly replied.

Ellie quickly dropped her backpack and began looking for a tool to open the hole wider. It was only a matter of seconds before she had a scrapping trowel in her hand and began scraping around the edge of the hole.

"Come take a look at this!" Ellie told Mandi.

The others left Remy and André tied up next to the wall in the very capable hands of Mandi's 'friends' and stepped over. One at a time, each one of them looked inside the hole.

"It's the same hieroglyphics I saw on mom's notes," Suzi mentioned as she stayed back and let the others look. Everyone stopped what they were doing and looked back at Suzi.

"Honestly, Suzanna! Why you don't come to me with this stuff is beyond me." Ellie was still frustrated and frightened, but still relieved.

"I'm sorry, Mom. We just weren't sure what we were looking at," Suzi continued. "With all the discussions between you guys, we wanted to be sure before we told you about anything. It could've been nothing."

"That should have been up to us to decide, young lady! Besides, look what happened! You guys could've been killed!" Ellie retorted.

"But we weren't, thanks to Mandi!" Suzi smiled as she tried to deflect.

"Oh, girl! Don't bring me into this! Your mom is right. I

shouldn't have had to save you." Mandi glared at her god-daughter.

"Thank you, though, Aunt Mandi," Suzi replied with humility and sincerity.

"Yeah, seriously. Thanks, Aunt Mandi," Ty agreed.

Both Naeem and Emma also gave a wide-eyed nod and agreed.

Ellie quickly reverted back to archaeologist mode and began planning the excavation. "Okay, first, let's get back to the camp and call the authorities on these two. Then, let's get a digging crew up here as early as tomorrow morning."

"Ellie, wait. We can't." Mandi stopped her, and then, from the shadows, the two men who had helped capture Remy and André walked up behind her.

"Fadil?" Naeem looked amazed. "Is that you?"

Fadil bowed his head and smiled. "Yes, my young friend."

Naeem looked at Ty. "Ha! Who knew? Great baklava *and* a ninja all in one!"

Fadil laughed. "No, my boy. I am Medjay." Fadil placed his hand over his heart and, again, bowed his head.

Ellie looked around at the entire situation. Her kids had been kidnapped, her best friend was some secret Medjay, there was a huge find only feet away from her she couldn't touch, and suddenly, she missed her wise and intuitive husband.

"Okay, well, first things first. Let's get these two back to camp. Would someone please call the authorities?" she sighed.

"Dr. Carruth, that has been taken care of," Fadil continued. "They are waiting for us."

"Oh, wow, okay. That's settled, then. Let's head back." Ellie looked at Mandi. "We can talk more when we get back to camp." She put her arm around Mandi's shoulder as they walked through the caverns toward the exit. "Did you really swoop in and kick butt?" Ellie asked playfully.

Fadil and Asim lifted Remy and André to their feet and walked them out. The other Medjay followed behind them.

Jake rounded up the kids and followed behind the others.

"Naeem, your dad is waiting for you just outside the cave," Jake said.

"Why didn't he come in with everyone else?" Naeem asked.

"Because he was standing guard with Nora," Jake replied.

"Standing guard with Nora? Is she some kind of Medjay, too? Is Papa a Medjay?" Naeem rattled off several questions.

"No, well, Nora is. But your dad is just a great dad who stood guard to protect his son," Jake smiled and placed his hand on Naeem's shoulder.

A short time later, as they approached the opening of the cave, Ahmal saw his son. He ran to Naeem and knelt down. "My son! Dear Allah! Are you alright?" Ahmal looked over every inch of his son.

"Yes, Papa. I am okay. I know . . . I am grounded." Naeem dropped his head. He knew he was in real trouble this time.

"Well, maybe we won't tell your mother this time," Ahmal continued. "I think she would be as mad at me for letting you out of my sight as she would be with you. So, maybe we keep this one to ourselves."

Naeem flung his arms around his father's neck and held on tight. Ahmal was so glad to see Naeem alive that he hugged his son tightly and was afraid to let go.

"We should probably get going," Suzi said to Jake.

"Yeah, come on, everybody, let's go," Jake agreed.

As they walked back across the desert toward camp, "That boy is never leaving my sight again." Ahmal said to Jake.

Jake laughed and patted his old friend on the back. "Now, now. Weren't you curious as a boy?"

Ahmal looked at Jake. "Yes, and that is why he's never leaving my sight. I was *always* in some sort of trouble."

"Well, at least he comes by it honestly," Jake chuckled.

23

As promised, the authorities were waiting on the outskirts of the camp, and they were not alone. Count Menkura and his assistant, Timmons, stood beside a black Bentley. Two Cairo police cars flanked each side of the Bentley, with several police officers. They were leaving nothing to chance. These were international criminals who Interpol wanted. Neither Egypt nor the Medjay were going to let them slip away.

Mandi, Fadil, and their colleague, Hakim, walked the prisoners up the hill to the waiting authorities.

Mandi hugged her father. "My dear Mandisa, you have saved our secret." Count Menkura placed his hands on her cheeks. He was always so proud of his daughter. "The society owes you a great debt, my dear."

"It was an honor, Father, as always," Mandi replied.

Fadil walked over to Count Menkura. "Sir, we still need to replace the artifact back to its home. If you can have the authorities take these men, we will take care of that task."

"Yes, yes, of course." Count Menkura motioned to the authorities. "Captain, if you would please?"

"Right away." The captain continued, "Sergeant, if you would take Remy Cobb with you. We will take the Frenchman with us. I have a few questions for Mr. Gagnon regarding an Interpol matter."

The police captain placed André in the back of the squad car and shut the door. He climbed into the front seat, while another officer walked around and sat beside André in the back.

As the police car began to drive off, the captain turned toward the back seat and pointed his gun at André. "Mr. Gagnon, for his own safety, the officer next to you is not carrying a weapon. If you attack him or make any sudden moves, I will shoot you where you sit. Is that understood?"

"Yes . . . " André Gagnon sarcastically glared back at the captain.

"Good. I'm glad we understand one another," the captain replied.

The two police cars drove away from camp towards Cairo, where André Gagnon and Remy Cobb would face severe charges of crimes against Egypt, kidnapping, as well as numerous unrelated Interpol charges that awaited them.

Mandisa looked at her father, Fadil, and Hakim. "I know the bracelet needs to be replaced, and I will handle that myself. But there are a few things I need to take care of first." Mandi continued, "Father, I will meet you in Cairo tomorrow evening."

"Of course, my dear," he replied.

Mandi looked at her Medjay brethren, "Fadil, for security reasons, if you and Hakim wouldn't mind staying in camp for the evening, we can take care of Nefertiti tomorrow," she asked.

Fadil looked over to Hakim, and they agreed. "Yes, Mandisa. We will stay with your crew tonight. I feel better being close by."

"I agree! I would feel better, too." Count Menkura patted Fadil on the back. "Thank you."

"Mandisa, we will let you say goodbye to your father. It is good to see you as always, Count. Thank you for your continued dedication to our cause," said Fadil.

Count Menkura placed his hand over his heart and bowed his head. Fadil and Hakim returned the gesture and walked back down the hill toward base camp.

"Mandisa, my dear, can you be certain the secret of the Medjay will be safe?" The Count was concerned. The Medjay had been virtually undetected for thousands of years.

"I am positive, Father. I will, of course, discuss this with Ellie and the team. But I'm sure you know, as I do, that she will keep our secret," Mandi continued. "As far as the others . . . I trust Ahmal with my life. And Jake, well, he is just like his aunt. He can be trusted."

"And the crew?" the count asked.

"The only crew members that knew what was going on were Medjay themselves. Nora made sure of that," Mandi explained.

"Good." Count Menkura then walked to the back door of his car. "It appears Malcolm Maldroon and his network of associates are behind all of this," he admitted.

"Is he still in control of the Western European Antiquities Network?" Mandi asked.

"Maldroon would sooner die than give up his control of that organization. Nasty, nasty man!" he replied, then climbed into the back seat of his Bentley.

Mandi blew a kiss and waved goodbye to her father.

24

Later that afternoon, the sun was setting, the air was getting cooler, and the smell of dinner filled the air. It had been a really long day for everyone.

"I smell garlic!" Tyler noticed.

"My dad's assistant cooked again tonight," Emma responded.

"NICE!" Ty and Naeem replied in unison.

"By the smell of it, dinner should be ready any minute," Emma said as she pushed Suzi slightly with her elbow.

"Oh, yeah, excellent," Suzi acknowledged, with what seemed to Emma as minimal enthusiasm.

"Ha! There's the bell!" Naeem exclaimed.

"Right on time!" Tyler rubbed his hands together and took a big sniff of the food's aroma.

The two boys ran off towards the mess tent. The excitement of the day had them famished.

Emma looked at Suzi. "Are you okay?"

"Oh, yeah. I'm good," Suzi responded, snapping out of her daze.

Emma could see her friend was preoccupied, so she decided to stay back with Suzi for a little while. "Do you want me to bring you any dinner?" she asked.

"Oh, no thanks. I'm good. I'll get something to eat in a few minutes. You go ahead," Suzi said.

Emma stared at her friend, but Suzi insisted, "I promise I'll be in to eat in a little while. You go!"

"Okay, I'll go. But you know where to find me if you want to talk."

"I do. Thanks, Emma."

Emma stood to leave but paused to look back at her friend. Suzi waved her off. "Go, I'll be right behind you."

Emma turned to head into the tent. Just as she was about to turn the corner, she glanced back again and went inside.

The summer evening air was crisp but pleasant. Suzi pulled her jacket together and zipped it. She had only been sitting alone for a few minutes when her brother walked up. He sat a plate of food next to her. "I figured you'd be out here a while. Thought you might want to eat before everything got cold."

"Thanks," Suzi picked up the plate and began moving her food around with the fork.

"Do you want to talk?" Tyler asked.

"No, not yet. Maybe later."

Tyler stood up. "Okay." He began to walk back towards the mess tent but turned back to his sister. "Eat!"

Suzi smiled at her brother. "Okay, I will, *Mom*."

Tyler laughed and walked away. "Yeah, well, don't make me tell *Mom* that you're not eating."

Meanwhile, Ellie, Asim, Ahmal, Jake, and Nora waited for Mandi to join them in the research tent.

"Asim, I need answers." Ellie continued, "I mean, I need to know everything!"

"And you will, but I must wait until Mandi arrives. Hopefully, it will be—"

At that moment, Mandi entered the tent. "Hi everyone."

Ellie simply looked at her friend. No words were necessary. Mandi sat in the chair next to the research table. One by one, the others grabbed a chair and sat around Mandi, waiting for further explanation of the day's events.

"Ellie," Asim began, "Nora and I are *sleeper* members of the Society. We only observe and come into use when the need arises. Like today." He continued, "Approximately six other members on *this* digging crew are sleepers as well."

"But Nora . . . you're English," Jake remarked.

"Yeah, sort of," Nora acknowledged. "I was *raised* in England, but my mom was French, and my father was Egyptian and a high-ranking member of The Medjay. After his death a few years ago, I joined the Society."

Mandi leaned forward and rested her elbows on her knees. "Listen carefully." She continued, "I, *we*, were sent here to protect the location of Nefertiti's resting place."

"Why?" Jake interrupted.

"Jake, please, let her finish." Ellie placed her hand on her nephew's knee to reassure him. "I'm sure there is an explanation." Ellie knew Jake was still sore about being railroaded with his calculations. But Mandi needed to be allowed to explain herself.

"As you know, in 1300's B.C., during Akhenaten's reign, there was a lot of speculation as to why and how Nefertiti disappeared from any record." Mandi stood and grabbed the simple wooden box from her backpack.

"If you'll recall, our legend says that priests sought to hide her from Akhenaten as soon as she was banished. They were afraid he would try to kill her. The necklace and bracelet that belonged to her favorite daughter were buried there with her. They cursed the bracelet to make sure that she was left to rest in peace and so that Akhenaten's followers didn't try to destroy her or her tomb." Mandi opened the box and revealed the beautiful purple pouch that contained Nefertiti's bracelet. "Somehow, at some point, it seems this bracelet was removed along with a few other small items in her possession, probably by grave robbers centuries later, who didn't realize what or *who* they'd found. Over the years, we've found these items and unsure where she was buried, we placed them in a small room near King Tut. Even though she was not his mother, that was as close as we could get to her whereabouts. Our forefathers kept her burial location secret and took it to the grave with them. As they all died, so did the location of her burial chamber. Until this bracelet popped up, that is."

Mandi carefully pulled the bracelet pouch from the box. "Ellie, you know I would never jeopardize the integrity of any archaeological dig. But this site, this location…" Mandi paused, "it can never be discovered. I have to get this bracelet back to… Wait, who is that? Is there someone out there?" Mandi looked toward the door of the tent.

Nora and Asim walked to the door and pulled back the flap of the tent. There stood Suzi, trembling in the cool evening air. "Suzanna Ellen Carruth! You have got to be kidding me!" Ellie was furious. "After everything that happened today, I cannot believe you are out there in the cold snooping . . . again!"

"I'm really sorry, Mom. But I had a good reason this time."

"Aunt Ellie, I don't mean to interfere," Jake whispered to his aunt, "but I distinctly remember Dad telling me all kinds of stories like this about you. Apparently, you were relentless."

Ellie glared back at her nephew for a moment. "Fine. Get in here out of the cold. I thought you were at the mess tent with everyone else eating." Ellie pulled a seat up for Suzi to sit down.

"I couldn't eat." Tears began to fill Suzi's eyes. "Mom, was Remy Cobb there the day Dad and Grampa died?"

Taken back by Suzi's question, suddenly Ellie realized why Suzi had been sitting out there all this time. Suzi and her dad were extremely close, and she was devastated when he died. Ellie recognized Remy when they turned him over to the Medjay in the cave. "So, he told you?" Ellie knelt down in front of her daughter.

"Yes, he said he was actually on the plane with them when it went down." Suzi looked down at her hands in her lap.

Ellie took her daughter's hand. "I understand you're upset, but maybe we can have this conversation a little later. Is that okay with you?"

"I guess so." Suzi wiped the tears from her eyes.

Nora handed Suzi a tissue. "How much did you hear kiddo?"

"Pretty much everything. I saw Aunt Mandi leave Fadil and Hakim, and I followed her here."

Mandi laughed. "Girl … we have *got* to talk."

Suzi blushed.

Mandi leaned into Suzi. "Doodle, we are going to allow you to stay, but you have to understand that anything you hear in here must *always* remain confidential!"

Suzi looked at her mom, Mandi, and Asim and awkwardly raised her right hand, "I swear."

Asim turned to Ellie. "We must return this bracelet; no one must know about this site. If this location falls into the wrong hands, Egypt could be cursed with disease and despair, and there will be little we can do about it."

Mandi turned toward Jake and Ahmal. "Jake, I am so sorry. I felt terrible about having to railroad you. Yes, your calculations and maps were excellent, as they always are. I watched you create the exact spot. But I needed to push you all in the wrong direction so I could use *your correct* map to slip in and replace the bracelet. Then, I needed to discredit your findings so no one would return here. I needed them to think this dig site was a bust," Mandi explained. "Again, Jake, I am really sorry."

"Why didn't you just tell me all this from the beginning?" Ellie asked Mandi.

Asim spoke for her. "Because our people have been protecting Egypt's deepest and darkest secrets for generations, centuries..."

" . . . It is a *'secret'* society," Mandi interrupted. "We had hoped to take care of the matter *in-house*, with no complications."

The group of adults looked in Suzi's direction. "Well, that didn't exactly work out, did it?" Jake commented.

"Ohh, fine. I said I was sorry already . . . geez!" Suzi retorted.

Ellie sighed. "Alright, what do you need from us?"

25

The morning sun was particularly bright as camp came to life. It wasn't the usual hustle and bustle of getting gear together or directives from team leaders. Nora and Asim told the crew as a group that the information they had received was inaccurate and that the dig would be postponed indefinitely. Asim apologized to everyone and assured the entire crew they would receive full pay for the work they had been scheduled to do. This seemed to make the men extremely happy. They could go home to their families a month early—with pay! Smiles spread across the faces of the diggers as they packed up their belongings and began loading the trucks.

In the research tent, Suzi sat at the desk, looking through her own documents and information on Nefertiti. She looked up at her mom, Jake, and Mandi, who had been combing through data and documents pertaining to the location and discovery of Nefertiti. "Hey, so . . . , something else happened in the cave yesterday, something really weird," Suzi casually mentioned.

"Oh, yeah? What was that?" Jake responded while sifting through a box of maps.

"I think we saw Nefertiti herself," Suzi said. "In the corridor."

Mandi dropped an armful of books and stood there staring at Suzi.

"I'm sorry; what did you say, honey?" Ellie asked.

"I said I think we actually saw Nefertiti, but she was, like, a ghost or something."

"What do you mean, like a ghost or something?" Jake also stopped what he was doing, giving his cousin his full attention.

Mandi pushed away the books she'd dropped at her feet and sat on the corner of the table next to Suzi while Jake and Ellie stood and stared at her.

"Honey, tell us what you mean by that," said Ellie.

"Well, the whole thing was sort of weird. Before we met those two Neanderthals, a bunch of crazy things happened." Suzi continued, "Not long after we had gotten deep into the cavern, it got weird. Our flashlights all flickered, and then all four of them died. Like, completely. Luckily, Tyler had a bunch of glow sticks in his backpack. Then, the hair on the back of our necks stood up, and it got seriously cold . . . I mean *really* cold. The kind of cold where you can see your breath. The smell was awful. Moldy and almost smelled like *death* or something. Then, the craziest thing of all happened. A ton of dust and sand flew up, and this woman appeared. I think it was Nefertiti's ghost! Oh, man, she was beautiful! She was long and slim. She wore a big gold headpiece and a beautiful blue and gold necklace."

Mandi reached over, grabbed the wooden box, and pulled out the purple pouch. "Suzi, did the necklace look like this?" She carefully exposed enough of the bracelet for Suzi to see its details.

"Yes! Exactly like that!" Suzi continued. "But she seemed sad, like she was upset about something. She paced back and forth, rubbing her wrist and crying." Then it occurred to Suzi, "Maybe she was looking for the bracelet *you* have!"

Ellie, Mandi, and Jake all looked at one another in disbelief. Then, Mandi spoke, "In all my years of working with the Society, working as the tending Egyptologist on countless digs, and exploring on my own, I have never encountered anything like this."

Curious, Ellie reached over and grabbed a document from under a stack of notebooks and papers. She remembered something she had found odd when she was reading through the case study before they left the United States. It was a statement from an old Bedouin shepherd, after an attack on his tribe during the night, by a group of desert bandits. It was in the file because it made mention of an object that possibly belonged to Nefertiti. The archaeological community was always vigilant with any and all chatter regarding antiquities found or sold on the black market, as well as any crimes related to these artifacts. The report found its way into the hands of Dr. Nasar, who accidentally included it in the files he sent to Ellie Carruth.

"Take a look at this." Ellie showed the document to Jake and Mandi.

"Wait, is that the police report about those shepherds?" Suzi asked.

Ellie just rolled her eyes. "Yes, dear. It is."

Suzi stood up and looked on, as the adults reviewed the accounts from the tribal elder. "Mom, I bet that was her."

"I agree," her mother confirmed.

Mandi slowly sat in the chair next to the table, breathless. "I would *love* to meet her!"

"Alright, so we know she is there. And she obviously wants her property back." Jake continued, "Mandi, you're planning to be the one to return it, correct? Maybe she'll show herself again."

Mandi looked up at Jake. "Maybe."

For the next few hours, the four of them continued to sort through the files, documents, and maps. They needed to destroy any mention of her existence and where she might be found. The dig needed to be a bust, with no evidence to the contrary.

Soon, the lunch bell rang, and what was left of the crew began to file into the mess tent. The four of them headed out for lunch and met Asim and Ahmal along the way. Mandi pulled Suzi off to the side.

"Doodle, I have a question for you, but you need to keep it to yourself, at least until later," Mandi said.

"Um, sure. Okay, what's up?" Suzi replied.

"I wondered if you would like to go back into the cave with me this afternoon to return the bracelet?" Mandi continued. "I mean, I'd understand if it's a bit too scary but . . . "

Suzi's eyes lit up as she interrupted Mandi, "Hooollly . . . are you serious? Yes! Yes! Please, oh, please!"

"Well, it would be nice to share it with you. Besides, I have a feeling Nefertiti likes you. I think she trusts you," Mandi continued. "We will be escorted by Fadil and Hakim, of course, as well as a couple other members of the Society, to post guard outside of the cave."

"Woo hoo! Yesss!" Suzi was so excited she could barely contain herself.

Mandi laughed and said, "Alright, it's settled. But remember," Mandi placed her finger to her lips. "Shhh."

"So, what exactly will we do once we're inside the cave?" Suzi asked, as she bounced all the way to the mess tent.

"Well, we will need to locate her chamber, specifically."

"I may have an idea about that," Suzi interrupted again. "I think there is a clue in that hole we found!"

"I agree." Mandi continued, "Then we'll present her with her bracelet, using an ancient prayer from the Book of the

Dead."

"What prayer? Book of the Dead!" Suzi squealed.

"Yes, the Book of the Dead, and I have that covered." Mandi smiled.

"And what about Mom? I'm not sure she'll let me do this!" Suzi stopped in her tracks.

"I got that part covered, too," Mandi replied with a smile and a wink, as she put her arm around her goddaughter's shoulder, and they walked into the meal tent.

Everyone at lunch was all smiles. The diggers, tech crews, scientists, and all who were still there. Even Nora had a huge smile on her face, as she sat with the crew she worked so closely with. Ahmal decided to eat with Emma, Tyler and Naeem. He usually ate with the diggers but chose to eat with his son and his friends today. Jake and Asim sat with Ellie. Ellie laughed at the stories Jake and Asim shared about their fun times working with Ellie's husband, Jason. There was a good vibe all around. The dig was a bust, and they would go home empty-handed, but no one seemed to mind. It all seemed right in some way.

26

Shortly after lunch, the remaining diggers left camp, except for those few who were members of the Society of the Medjay. They stayed behind to make sure the camp was secure and that no further issues would arise from members of the Western Europe Antiquities Network. By now, they knew Malcolm Maldroon, the leader of the network, would know his men had been arrested, and he would not be happy about it.

At 2:00 p.m., Mandi went to the Carruth tent where Suzi and her mom had been having a long talk about Remy Cobb, her dad and grandfather, and most importantly, her insatiable meddling.

"You ready?" Mandi asked as she poked her head inside the tent.

"Yep," Ellie replied. "She's ready to go."

Suzi could do little else other than grin. She was about to be a part of something very special.

Ellie walked with her daughter and Mandi to the edge of the camp, where Fadil, Hakim, and two other Medjay were waiting.

"Please be safe!" Ellie said and hugged her daughter. "Please watch her . . . you know how she is," Ellie said with a chuckle as she hugged her best friend.

"They will be safe," Fadil remarked. "Nora is going to stay back with a few others to make sure you are all safe here in camp."

"Thanks, Fadil," Ellie replied.

Suzi looked back over her shoulder at her mother. "Love you, Mom!"

"Love you too. Now go!" Ellie smiled as she waved them off.

As the group walked away toward the cave, Ellie was unusually calm. She knew this would be good for her daughter; although, she wasn't too thrilled at how they'd gotten to this point. Ellie decided to stay at the edge of camp and wait. She could see them going and coming from there. She found a large boulder and made herself comfortable. Tyler walked up, climbed onto the rock, and sat next to his mother.

"Where are they going?" he asked.

"They are going to return the bracelet," Ellie answered.

"Suzi is going too?"

"Yep."

"And you're okay with that?"

"Yep."

Tyler looked at his mother. "And you wonder why she is the way she is."

"What is that supposed to mean?" Ellie smiled and looked at her son. She already knew the answer.

"You know . . . " Ty snickered.

"Well, you just never mind," Ellie said and nudged her son.

"I'm all packed. So, I'll just wait here with you until they get back." Tyler smiled.

"I'd like that." Ellie put her arm around her son, gave him a nice, tight hug, and kissed him on the cheek.

A short time later, Mandi, Suzi, and their small group reached the cave's entrance. Two Medjay posted themselves there to stand guard. Fadil and Hakim stepped in, lit their flashlights, and looked around for trouble before motioning the "all clear" for Mandi and Suzi to enter the cave.

Hakim looked at Suzi and smiled, "Lead the way, my child," and then motioned for her to take the lead. They knew she knew the more direct route through the cave.

Suzi and Mandi wandered through the cavern corridors, Fadil and Hakim following closely behind.

When they got to the drawings on the wall, Suzi motioned to the others, "This way."

Eventually, they found themselves in the same spot they had been the day before.

"There's the hole," Suzi said.

Fadil and Hakim opened their backpacks and pulled out a few tools to start trying to open the hole wider when Suzi noticed a stone that appeared to be set into the wall by itself. Oddly, it was set in a wall that was mostly flat rock.

"Wait . . . " Suzi walked over to the stone. "Aunt Mandi, this looks like a push lever!"

"I think so too!" Fadil agreed.

Hakim walked over to the stone and gave it a hard push. It was tight and stiff, but he managed to push the stone inward until they heard it release some sort of latch.

Suzi's eyes were wide open. "Woah!" Suzi exclaimed, as they noticed the wall to their left began to shift and move.

"Dear Allah!" Fadil agreed.

Mandi took a deep breath as she and Hakim pushed hard to open the door enough so they could enter the room.

They each squeezed through the cracked door and entered the chamber one by one.

"This is it, Aunt Mandi! This is it!" Suzi looked around at the beautifully preserved walls. "These hieroglyphics match Mom's notes."

"I think this may be the entrance to her resting chamber," Mandi replied.

Suzi, still wide-eyed, looked at her godmother. "She's here. I just know it!"

"I believe so, Doodle!" Mandi looked at the markings and messages on the walls. "Yep, I believe so."

"Would you look at these inscriptions?" Fadil said, looking around the room in amazement. He rested his arm on a statue of Isis that stood in the middle of the room. As he put his weight down, another door cracked open.

"Haa!" Suzi squealed.

Hakim laughed. "I think you have found her resting place, my friend."

Mandi pointed her flashlight inside the room to look around. At first glance, it seemed like any other resting room she'd ever seen. Once inside, she noticed how unassuming and subtle the room was. Beautiful statues and chests flanked the sarcophagus on each side. It wasn't elaborate, just simple and beautiful.

Suzi breathed heavily as she followed Mandi into the room. Fadil and Hakim stopped at the doorway.

"My dear Mandisa, out of respect, we will wait out here. This is your task, not ours," Fadil said.

But before they could step back, a burst of dust and sand whirled around them and stung their faces as it swirled. Suzi quickly pulled her baseball hat low to cover her face. Mandi closed her eyes and pulled her blue scarf over her nose. Suddenly, it became ice cold in the chamber.

"She's back!" Suzi exclaimed. "Holy crap! She's here!"

Mandi looked up and stood completely still. Both Fadil and Hakim quickly knelt on one knee and bowed their heads. The smell of mold and dirt began to fill the room. Appearing before them was the most beautiful creature they had ever seen. The apparition was long and sleek. Clearly a woman, her hair was black as coal, and her piercing brown eyes looked down upon them. A gold crown, suitable for an Egyptian queen, sat elegantly on her head. Around her neck was the gold and lapis necklace Suzi had described. And true to Suzi's word, it matched the bracelet Mandi had in her possession.

"It is time, Mandisa," Fadil whispered softly.

"Time for what?" Suzi asked quietly.

"The prayer," Fadil whispered. "She must present the bracelet to the queen and apologize for the theft."

"Oh, right." Suzi quickly understood. She kept her head low and bowed as she slowly stepped backward towards Fadil and Hakim.

Mandisa pulled the small, simple wooden box from her backpack. Then, she knelt before the queen and began to recite the prayer of forgiveness in the ancient Egyptian language. She opened the box, laid it a few feet in front of her, and continued to repeat the prayer. The queen knelt down in front of Mandisa and placed her right hand on Mandi's shoulder. She then took the bracelet from the box and stood before them. All four of them continued to kneel with their heads bowed.

"Thank you," Nefertiti quietly whispered in her ancient tongue, and then, with a soft whirl of wind, she was gone.

Dazed, the four of them sat there and looked around at one another in complete awe of what had just happened. Finally, Mandisa broke out into a soft laughter. "Can you believe what just happened?"

"Holy crap!" Suzi chimed in with laughter as well. "No one is going to believe this!"

"My child, I am afraid you must never speak of this," Fadil spoke with a direct and serious tone.

"He's right, Doodle," Mandi agreed. "This was amazing and something we are never likely to forget or experience again. But I am afraid Fadil is correct. Remember what we told you before. NO ONE must ever know what happened here. I will have to brief my father and the elders of our Society on the events that took place, but unfortunately, this is a secret only you can have."

"Oh, right," Suzi remembered her promise. "I get it. It's sad, though, that it has to be this way."

"I agree, Miss Suzi," Hakim spoke up. "But you must remember your promise."

"Yes, sir. I promise." Suzi clearly understood the need for secrecy.

"Excellent!" Fadil said. "Now, who is up for some of that leftover pie from last night before they get rid of it?"

Suzi was quick to respond. "Me! Definitely Me!"

The four of them gathered their things and began to walk out of the chamber. Being the last one to step out of the room, Suzi looked back at the beautiful room she could never speak of again. "Sleep well, Queen Nefertiti," Suzi whispered. Suddenly, a small swirl of dust and sand emerged, and Nefertiti's face appeared. She bowed her head to Suzi. Then, as quickly as she appeared, she disappeared.

Suzi caught her breath and looked out the door at Mandi, then looked back into the room. "Woah!" Suzi whispered to herself, as she walked out of the room.

"You okay, Doodle?" Mandi asked.

"Yep, I'm good," Suzi smiled.

Hakim pulled the statue of Isis forward, closing the door to the main chamber. The four of them stood there staring at the door that led to the most amazing sight any of them had ever seen.

Snapping out of her stare, "Okay, let's go," Mandi whispered.

"Right, let us go." Fadil pulled himself together as well.

After passing through the forward room and back into the cave hallway, Fadil and Hakim pushed the cracked door to the chamber and closed it tightly. The men gathered sand into a pile, then poured a little water on it, to create a muddy mix. They placed the muddy sand in the crevices around the stone that opened the door. Next, they filled the hole in the wall with rocks and muddy sand. They disguised both the hole and the release lever, in case anyone else found their way into the sacred cave.

"Alright, looks good, guys," Mandi said.

They made their way through the cavern to the entrance of the cave. There, they met up with the two guards, and all six of them headed back down the hill towards camp.

Ellie and Tyler still sat perched on the boulder at the edge of camp. In the distance was Count Menkura, leaning against the hood of his Bentley, Timmons by his side, of course.

"Hey, Mom." Suzi smiled and hugged her mom. "Thanks for letting me go."

"Well, I knew this was something you needed to be a part of," Ellie said.

"Everything go okay?" Ty asked.

"Yep," Suzi replied.

"She did a wonderful job!" Mandi acknowledged, then looked up the hill at her father. "I'll catch up with you guys later. Oh, and save me some of that apple pie!"

"Definitely! We're heading over there now!" Ellie replied.

Fadil and Hakim followed Mandisa up the road to where Count Menkura waited.

The Carruths headed back to camp. "I'm starving," Suzi remarked. "Did they save anything from lunch besides pie?"

"I'm not sure, but I would guess so, as long as we still have people here," Ellie said.

Although the mess tent itself had been taken down, a small sandwich station was set up for the remaining crew to take food on the road with them back to Cairo.

"Yes! Sandwiches!" Tyler exclaimed.

Suzi packed herself a couple of sandwiches for the trip back to Cairo, then grabbed a slice of apple pie. Apple was definitely her favorite. She walked up the hill at the edge of camp and looked back at the cave where they had been wandering around, were nearly killed, and had found the mysterious Queen Nefertiti. She sighed as she sat her paper plate and fork down beside her, nothing but crumbs left on the plate, of course. A few moments later, Mandi joined Suzi on the hill. "You okay, Doodle?"

"Oh, yeah, definitely."

"You look like you're back in that cave," Mandi said as she sat down next to Suzi with her own pie and began to eat.

"Kinda," Suzi admitted. "I'm not in trouble with the Medjay, am I? I mean, like, I'm not going to be killed in my sleep because I know too much?"

Mandi looked at her goddaughter and laughed. "No! Why on earth would you think that?" she continued, shaking her head. "You watch too much TV."

Suzi looked at her godmother wide-eyed. "Um, I don't know. Maybe because you three came into that cave like three stealthy assassins when we were kidnapped, then swore me to secrecy."

"Well, we were worried. And with good cause! You guys could've been killed," Mandi scolded. "Those guys, particularly André Gagnon, are really bad news."

"I know. But we had no idea they were even there." Suzi tried to defend their actions; however, Mandi was not having it.

"That's just it . . . you never know."

"Aunt Mandi?"

"Yep?" Mandi replied as she stuffed the last bite of pie into her mouth.

"I wonder why Nefertiti was so upset about a simple bracelet."

"Well, legend has it, at least among the Medjay, that the bracelet and necklace belonged to her daughter."

Suzi looked at her godmother with the look Mandi had seen many times over—one of intrigue and interest.

Mandi continued, "Do you recall the story of Akhenaten and how he converted the religion of the entire country to serving only the Sun Disc God, Aten?"

"Yeah," Suzi replied.

Mandi went on. "Well, the queen's favorite daughter died. No one really knows why. Legend says that the queen was devastated and depressed and abandoned the Aten religion altogether, as a result. Akhenaten was furious and banished her. Some priests were said to have hidden her away until she finally died of despair and depression. They buried her with the bracelet and necklace that once belonged to her beloved daughter and placed a curse on the jewelry so no one, especially Akhenaten, would disturb her. Once the bracelet had been removed, it had to be replaced by the 6th full moon, or the curse would affect all of Egypt."

"Oooh, that's why we had to go *today* by sundown! Tonight would've been the 6th full moon," Suzi said.

"That is correct," Mandi replied.

Suzi looked down at the cave. This would be an experience

she would never forget. "Thanks for trusting me, Aunt Mandi."

Mandi hugged her goddaughter. "You are very welcome, Doodle."

"So, what happened to all those papers that say where she is?" Suzi asked.

"Well, 'officially,' we had a 'mysterious' fire in our research tent. An aid accidentally left the lantern too close to the file table," Mandi said with a wink. "Unofficially, we put them in the campfire."

"You burned them?" Suzi looked at her godmother. "You burned all that history?"

"We had to," Mandi replied. "We couldn't risk anyone finding any evidence pointing to her location."

"I mean, I get it. But ugh! All that work!"

Mandi put her arm around Suzi's shoulder. "Let's head back down and get packed up."

By sunset, the entire crew had packed everything and was ready to roll out. One by one, Suzi, Tyler, Naeem, and Emma made their way to the line of jeeps and trucks that were loaded and ready to head back.

"This has been one crazy trip," Ty exclaimed.

Naeem glared at his friend and replied, "Yes, and I do not care to repeat it."

"I can honestly say I have never experienced anything like this in my entire life, that's for sure," Emma agreed.

"I think Papa is going to put me on a short leash for a while," Naeem admitted.

"You're awfully quiet." Emma looked at Suzi. "Are you okay?"

"Oh, yeah, definitely!" Suzi continued, "I just see it all differently."

"How so?" Emma asked.

"Well, think about it . . . Yes, we ran into a slightly dangerous situation, but . . . "

"Slightly?" Naeem interrupted.

Suzi laughed. "Okay, a very dangerous situation." She looked at her friend and smiled. "But look at what we saw. Look what we helped to accomplish."

"It's true," Emma said.

"But we can't tell anyone," Tyler said reluctantly.

"No, but it's something the four of us will always have together," Suzi said.

"It is going to be so boring again when you two leave," Naeem said.

"Hey! What am I? Chopped liver?" Emma retorted.

"My apologies." Naeem smiled, placed his hand over his chest, and bowed his head.

Suzi, Tyler, and Emma laughed, and then Suzi and Ty threw their bags into the back of their Jeep. "Hey, Mom!" Ty yelled.

"Yes, son, what is it?" Ellie yelled back from the back of the convoy.

"Can Naeem and Emma ride with us?" Ty asked.

"I'm not sure we have the room!" Ellie replied.

Jake leaned over to his aunt. "Aunt Ellie, I can ride with Ahmal and Asim. That'll give you room in your Jeep."

"Well, if it's okay with their parents, I don't have a problem with it either," Ellie yelled back.

Ahmal and Asim walked up after they tossed their bags into the back of the jeep.

"Can we, Papa?" Emma pleaded.

"Yes, it is okay with me," Asim replied.

Ahmal looked at his son and raised his eyebrow. "I guess it is okay."

"YES!" Suzi exclaimed.

Before anyone could change their minds, they quickly crawled into the Jeep and buckled up. Fortunately, this big Jeep seated six because Mandi was also along for the ride.

As it was, they would not get into Cairo until very late. So, everyone quickly loaded into their respective vehicles and headed out. There was a quiet but almost relieved feeling in the caravan. Everyone traveling was either part of the scientific leadership, their families, or members of the Medjay. The sense of accomplishment, without a shred of evidence, was both enlightening and comforting.

Ellie looked over at Mandi, who was sitting in the passenger seat of the Jeep. "How will you keep people from stumbling into the cave again?"

"We are sending people out to place large boulders at the entrances to the cave," Mandi replied. "Including the one you all found cliffside." Mandi looked back at Suzi and Ty in the back seat.

"That won't be easy. That one literally is about eight feet up on the side of the hill," Ty remarked.

"We'll handle it!" Mandi winked.

27

In Cairo early the next day, the jeeps and trucks were unpacked from the trek home the night before, and it was time to say goodbye. Naeem and his dad always hated this part, but they loved it when the Carruths were there. "We will miss you, Dr. Carruth." Ahmal hugged his old friend.

"Are you ever going to call me Ellie?"

"It is not likely," Ahmal replied with a smile.

The Carruth clan was sad as well. Ty usually looked forward to getting home to his friends, but Naeem was also one of his best friends, and leaving Egypt was usually tough. The two shared a 'bro-hug' and secret handshake, then planned to catch up on social media next week.

Ellie hugged Mandi, and they, too, made plans to talk in the upcoming week. Ellie still had lots of questions. Jake said his goodbyes earlier because he had to catch an extremely early flight to New York. He decided to use the extra time off to visit his parents, which was something he rarely got the chance to do.

"Asim," Ellie said. "It was a pleasure meeting you. I'm sure Jason is pleased we were able to finally work together."

"Ellie, I am quite certain he got a laugh at how it all turned out," Asim admitted.

"He always encouraged Suzanna's inquisitive ways," Ellie continued. "But I'm sure he was holding his breath on this one."

Asim laughed. "I am sure he was!"

"Thank you, Asim. For everything!" Ellie hugged her new friend and colleague. "I'm sure we will meet again."

"I truly hope so," Asim smiled.

Tyler and Ellie climbed into the airport limo. Suzi hugged her new friend and the two locked pinky fingers.

"You have my social media, right?" Suzi asked.

"Yep, you have mine?" Emma replied.

"I do. Let's chat when I get home, okay?"

"Okay!" Emma said, and the two hugged again.

"Suz! Let's go! We don't want to miss the flight!" Ellie said.

"Okay," Suzi said as she climbed into the limo and went off. She waved goodbye to her new friend out of the back window. *It's okay*, she thought to herself. *We will definitely stay in touch.*

EPILOGUE

July, North Carolina

Tucked away in the study of the Carruth home, Suzi sat focused, reading from her laptop.

"Suz? Where are you, hon?" Ellie called out. "Suzi? Did you feed the horses this morning? It's your turn today!"

"I'm in the study," Suzi continued. "Yes, I fed them about thirty minutes ago."

"There you are. What are you doing?" Ellie stopped at the door.

"Just reading." Suzi looked up over the edge of her laptop, hoping her mother didn't decide to venture in.

"Okay, well, let's keep the screen time down to a minimum." Ellie went to walk away but stopped to look back in. "Oh, hey. Have you talked to Emma lately?"

"Yep . . . " Suzi kept her eyes glued to the computer. "We video-chatted for several hours last night."

Ellie stared at her daughter briefly, then cautiously walked away.

Making sure the coast was clear, Suzi pulled up the search engine she'd hidden when her mother came to the door. She typed . . . *"Western European Antiquities Network"* . . . *"Collin Carruth"* . . . *"Black Market Antiquities."*

. . . SEARCH . . .

MESSAGE FROM THE AUTHOR

I hope you enjoyed Nefertiti's Bracelet as much as I enjoyed introducing Suzi and Tyler's adventures to you. I look forward to bringing their next adventure, The Engineer's Timepiece, into your world. While Suzi continues to struggle with new evidence on the death of their father, Tyler and his cousin, Jake, find themselves in an extremely unusual predicament in very unfamiliar territory. They must rely on their wits, along with the help of family, an old wolf, and some of history's most notorious train robbers to find their way out.

For more updates and series information please visit DonnaFeraBooks.com.

ABOUT THIS SERIES

The series follows Suzi and Tyler Carruth, as they travel the globe with their mother, famed archaeologist Dr. Ellie Carruth, in search of the world's most elusive artifacts. The stories pick up one year after the untimely death of the father, who perished in a plane crash over the Peruvian Amazon. The young Carruth siblings find themselves navigating through a dangerous network of black market antique dealers who they suspect might be responsible for their father's death. With The Network at every turn, they must use their wit and intelligence to outsmart these ruthless antiquities dealers and help their mother secure these ancient relics.

ABOUT THE AUTHOR

Donna Fera's love of writing blossomed during her high school English class. As she grew up, she held two careers, a history teacher and a flight attendant. Her first project began as a single mom, while teaching and raising her two children. It wasn't until she left teaching and became a flight attendant that she was able to finish her first project, Nefertiti's Brace-let. She continued to write consistently on long layovers and her days off. It wasn't long before she had completed multiple books, and The Carruth Chronicles was born.